ABOUT THIS BOOK

How far are you willing to go to win back the person you love? For someone as desperate as Rayonus, the answer is pretty damn far.

For six hundred years, demon Rayonus Rixa has used the threat of his destructive power to fund his nomadic, mercenary lifestyle and hasn't had the time or inclination to care about someone other than himself. The day the demon hierarchy tasked him with a job unlike any other, that all changed, and in turn, he changed. Whether that was for the better was debatable until the moment he met the person who made him stop in his tracks.

Penelope Osbourne was unlike anyone he had ever met—sassy, beautiful, and a little crazy for her favorite TV angel. He knew she would be it for him. In Penelope, he finally found a future that didn't include death or general mayhem. Then, in typical demon fashion, he promptly screwed it up ten ways to Sunday.

With nothing left to lose, Rayonus sets out to do the impossible by any means necessary, and if that means he has to become a model citizen of Havenwood Falls, then that's what he'll do. For her, he will do anything.

HAVENWOOD FALLS BOOKS

Forget You Not by Kristie Cook

Old Wounds by Susan Burdorf

Fate, Love & Loyalty by E.J. Fechenda

The Winged & the Wicked by T.V. Hahn & Kristie Cook

Alpha's Queen by Lila Felix

Ink & Fire by R.K. Ryals

Lose You Not by Kristie Cook

Tragic Ink by Heather Hildenbrand

Nowhere to Hide by Belinda Boring

Flames Among the Frost by Amy Hale

Rock Me Gently by Susan Burdorf

From the Embers by Amy Miles

Defying Gravity by Kallie Ross

Break Me Not by Kristie Cook

How the Dead Lie by Stacey Rourke

The Lurkers Within by Danielle Bannister

The Collector: Awakening by Kristie Cook, R.K. Ryals, Belinda Boring & Nadirah Foxx

Addicted to You by Belinda Boring

Affliction Mine by C.J. Pinard

The Ward & the Wanderers by T.V. Hahn

Toil & Trouble by Melissa Wright

Of Salt and Stars by Seven Jane

Redefined by Morgan Wylie

Betrayal Among the Frost by Amy Hale

Forever Loyal by E.J. Fechenda

Fate's Demand by Emily Cyr

The Wu & the Wand by T.V. Hahn

A Demon's Redemption by JD Nelson

Also try the YA line, Havenwood Falls High; the historical paranormal line, Legends of Havenwood Falls; the darker, sexier side of town, Havenwood Falls Sin & Silk; and the local supernatural college, Sun & Moon Academy.

Stay up to date at www.HavenwoodFalls.com

BOOKS BY JD NELSON

Wicked Ways Series

A Night of Wickedness

All I Want For Christmas Are My Two Front Fangs: A Wicked Ways Companion Novel

Wolves Will Be Wolves

Too Cute To Spook: A Wicked Ways Companion Novel

Night Aberrations Series

Night Aberrations

The Fire within the Night

Stand Alone Novels

Control: A Tale of Desire

Havenwood Falls

Plans Laid Bare

Soul Laid Bare

A Demon's Redemption

A DEMON'S REDEMPTION

A HAVENWOOD FALLS NOVELLA

JD NELSON

To Nels, always Nels.

CHAPTER 1

*E*very demon has a breaking point, and as it turns out, my breaking point was the sixty-seventh time Penelope Osbourne told me to go fuck myself.

She didn't even ease me into it. She verbally pounced on me while I was waiting to cross the street at Main and Eighth, chewed me up, and spit me out as if I wasn't worth the effort it took to swallow. All I could do was stare as she stormed away, the fury and heat of a thousand suns in her usually cheerful brown eyes.

And, to think, before I came along, she used to be such a nice woman.

"How does one go about redeeming oneself?" I asked aloud, throwing myself onto the nearest bench and burying my head in my hands. I was tired, so tired, of trying and failing. My confidence was shaken to my core. And for me—hell, for any demon—that was really saying something.

To my surprise, someone answered my exhausted query. "In my experience, you start with flowers and work your way up to the hard stuff."

Mouth quirked into a suppressed grin, I looked up to find a violet-eyed woman with a sleek silver-blond bob smiling down at me. I hadn't realized anyone had been close enough to overhear me, but I guess I should've. This was Havenwood Falls, after all. I knew to expect the unexpected when dealing with its citizens.

Sliding over, I offered the lady a seat next to me on the park bench and asked, "Do you have much experience in redeeming yourself?"

She grinned as she sat. "No, but I do have experience with flowers. My sister, Reagan, and I own Fairy Tale Florists over on Fifth Street."

"Well, if you're willing to help me out of a hopeless, no chance of succeeding, ridiculously horrible situation, I'm willing to try anything." I stuck out my hand. "I'm Rayonus Rixa."

"Rhiannon Underwood. Nice to meet you, Rayonus."

"Likewise," I told her, genuinely meaning it. "So, tell me a little more about how this flowers-to-redemption thing works. Because for the life of me, I cannot get the hostile woman I love to see me as more than someone who has betrayed her trust."

"I saw that, and I have to ask—do you deserve to be seen as anything more than that?"

I sighed, staring down at my black leather boots, embarrassed, not for the first time, that I had been such a schmuck. "Truthfully, Rhiannon, in the beginning, I didn't."

She nodded in understanding. "But you're different now?"

"Decidedly so." I met her kind eyes. She was so easy to talk to; I felt compelled to tell her the truth. "I feel absolutely nothing but remorse for what I've done. I love her. I'll never do anything to hurt Penelope again."

And it was true. Every single word of it.

Seemingly satisfied with the honesty in my answer, Rhiannon said, "Well, Rayonus, I think I can help you. Or, at least, I can try."

Sighing in relief, I gave her a grateful smile. "You're too kind."

"Nonsense," she said, waving away my gratitude. "You can thank me when *and if* you get back into your Penelope's good graces."

"I will do that," I told her, suppressing another grin. I was going to like Rhiannon Underwood.

After a few more minutes of chatting, Rhiannon invited me to walk with her from the town square to her flower shop, a dark gray three-story Victorian with whimsical eggplant purple trim, complete with turrets and an odd, beguiling charm that made me feel instantly at home. The interior was just as delightful, with colorful butterflies and small chirping birds flying about the lush greenery and flowers in perfect harmony.

I stood still, nearly gaping at the enchanting sight. "This is lovely."

"Thank you," she said, gesturing to a petite brunette with striking blue-green eyes behind the counter. "Allow me to introduce my sister, Reagan Fairchild. Reagan, this is Rayonus Rixa."

"How do you do, Mr. Rixa?" Reagan asked.

"I am very well, now that your kind sister has agreed to help me in my quest to win back the heart of my beloved."

Brows raised, Reagan gave her sister a quizzical look and stuck a pencil behind her ear. "Has she? Then I wish you luck."

"I need all the luck I can get," I told her, noticing the *Help Wanted* sign displayed next to her. "And speaking of that, are you, by chance, still hiring?"

"Yes, we are. Are you in search of a job?"

I nodded. "Sadly, my job giving the occasional ghost tour doesn't quite allow me to pay my way. I've been living off my savings and staying with friends until something steadier comes along."

"Well, if you can be reliable and show up on time, I think Reagan and I can give you a shot," Rhiannon said. "On a trial basis, of course."

"Of course. Thank you. You don't know how much I appreciate everything you're doing for me."

She winked. "You should. This will give you the perfect opportunity to see your Penelope."

Grinning conspiratorially, I said, "I see you and I are of the same mind."

Interest piqued, Reagan fingered the fine pearls around her neck and asked, "Is Penelope your beloved?"

"Yes. It may be an impossible task, but I'm trying to earn back her trust, and hopefully, her regard."

Reagan nodded sagely. "Then you're going to need roses.

Rhiannon's arrangements have a way of changing even the hardest of hearts."

I retrieved my wallet from my back pocket and pulled out my debit card. "You'd better ring me up for a few dozen, because, after what I've done, this particular heart may be a little harder than most."

I left Fairy Tale Florists and headed home feeling both lighter and conflicted. While delivering flowers for the ladies would give me a much-needed chance to see Penelope outside of her job at the Chinese buffet, it was also just a front—one that made me feel like a great big douche for lying about my circumstances to the ladies to get the job. It was true I did need steady employment, but it was only for appearance's sake. I didn't need money. After six hundred years of devious deals and double-crossing demon activity, I'd amassed quite a bit of wealth and wouldn't be strapped for cash for the next millennium or so. What I was strapped for was a reason to stay in town. The more Penelope saw me around, making an effort to call Havenwood Falls my home and not just my occasional crash pad, the better.

I shook my head as I internally berated myself. It seemed funny to me now—the way I used to be. I had been the most cunning and deceptive demon I knew, save for a few megalomaniacal examples. There hadn't been a creature—demon, human, or otherwise—that I cared one fig about. Then I met Penelope, and everything started to change. I started to change. My priorities, once selfish and self-centered, were becoming focused on the one thing that really mattered —the sweet and funny half-demon woman that had no inkling she wasn't one hundred percent human.

Sadly, as much as I had wanted to do the right thing by her, my careless, reckless demon nature made a wreck of everything. Once I had gained everything I wanted in Penelope—her reluctant admiration, her trust—I traded it all away on a crazy roundabout plan that nearly got her killed because I was prone to go into every situation with guns blazing instead of thinking about what the outcome could end up being.

Kidnapping her? Taking her to be imprisoned (however temporarily) by a demon I knew wouldn't care if she ended up a casualty? I honestly didn't know what I had been thinking, and if she never forgave me, I wouldn't blame her.

CHAPTER 2

"*H*ey, Mrs. Claus! I'm home!" I yelled, opening the holiday-bedecked door of a house that had been painstakingly decorated more than a full month early.

The Homes for the Holidays tour was a big deal in Havenwood Falls. At least, that was what I was always told and retold by my benevolent benefactress when she deigned to speak to me.

My best incubus friend, Cameron DeSalle, and his Christmas-obsessed wife, Mavis, had been gracious enough to allow me to stay with them for almost a year, both here and at their apartment in Havenwood Village. As grateful as I was for the hospitality, the absolute best part about the arrangement was that I got to annoy Mavis pretty much all day, every day. Getting her riled up to the point she was angry enough to use her rarely seen ice demon abilities was one of my favorite pastimes. Though I have to say, those ice balls she'd learned to create hurt like a bitch when she aimed for my head.

"Oh, super," Mavis grouched, coming into the living room with a pink apron tied around her waist and a smudge of flour on her cheek. "It's you."

I grinned at the tiny blond beauty and used my thumb to wipe away the flour. "The one and only. Did you miss me, or did you and the elves keep yourselves occupied this morning?"

I grinned at her feisty little expression of indignation as she swatted my hand away. As much as I gave her shit for it and as bizarre as it was to see a demon so domestic, I really did love coming home to the extravagant Christmas display she'd created. I planned on helping to make it an even bolder one by hanging about a million and a half strands of sparkly lights outside after Halloween. She tolerated the very sight of me every day, so I figured, at the least, she deserved pretty lights to make up for it.

"Me? Miss you?" She harrumphed and headed back to the kitchen. "Yeah, I missed you—like a human misses the flu. What are you even doing here, Ray? I thought you were out for a walk."

"It's Rayonus," I corrected, teasing her with our usual argument over the use of my nickname. It was more fun with Penelope, but Mavis always did well in a pinch.

She rolled her eyes. "Fine. Rayonus."

"Thank you," I said, preening at my little battle won. "And I was out for a walk. But something quite unexpected happened while I was out."

"Penelope told you to go fuck yourself again?" she guessed. "She said she saw you this morning."

I took a freshly baked sugar cookie off a cooling sheet pan and popped a piece of it in my mouth. "No. Well, yes, but that's not that unexpected, is it?"

She pressed her lips together and let out a long-suffering sigh through her nose. "Not lately."

"So, what happened?" Cameron asked, walking into the kitchen to join us. He kissed his wife on the cheek and stole a cookie before lifting himself onto the opposite counter to watch her work.

Making myself comfortable on a barstool, I smiled at the pair. "I got a job today."

"Don't you already have a job?" Cam asked, dark brows furrowed over his amber-colored eyes.

"I do, but twice-a-week ghost tours aren't exactly keeping me in the lavish lifestyle I deserve."

"Lavish lifestyle?" Mavis asked. "How're you going to manage that? Are you planning on picking up Cameron's old line of work?"

Cam burst out laughing. "I don't think Rayonus would make a good escort. He lacks a certain . . . um, let's call it 'finesse.'"

She shrugged and cocked her head to the side as she examined me. "I don't know. Look at him, babe. The lean, muscled physique, the tight ass-hugging jeans, that one blue eye and one black demon eye— as much as I hate to say it, he's got that tall, dark, and intriguing thing going on. Who wouldn't jump at the chance to get him into bed?"

"Penelope, for one," Cam answered, jumping off the counter to pull her away from me. "And you, for a second. Have you forgotten what an asshole he is? You have to be nice to people to make the kind of money I made."

"You know, I am standing right here," I griped, though I was incredibly bemused at Mavis's surprisingly positive assessment of my appearance. "You'd think you guys would be more excited about the prospect of me moving out."

Mavis perked up. "Move out? You didn't mention moving out. Where are you working? When can you leave?"

I rolled my eyes. "Your caring and compassion for my feelings really know no bounds."

"Hey, I didn't kill my evil fake grandfather and buy this gigantic house with the money I inherited for no reason," she said. "I want to spend some uninterrupted time with my husband that you can't hear . . . or ridicule."

"Or critique," Cam added.

"So you can christen every piece of furniture in the house?" I asked. "You know, you could say I've been doing your future guests a great service by staying here."

"How do you know we haven't christened the furniture even with you living here?" Cam asked, wrapping his arms around his wife and planting more than a friendly kiss on her neck.

I shivered at the thought of the two naked demons on the settee where I read my copy of *Sun & Moon Tribune* every Sunday. "Can we get back to my job at Fairy Tale Florists?"

Cam's mouth dropped open. "You're working for Reagan and Rhiannon?"

I nodded. "I'll be delivering flowers on a trial basis, but regardless of whether it works out or not, I'm moving back into your old apartment in Havenwood Village. I should have done it already. I signed the lease right after you bought the house."

Mavis gaped at me, her blue-gray eyes wide with shock. "You cannot be serious. Tell me you're not serious." She groaned. "Penny is going to flip her shit when she sees you've moved in next door to her."

"She can flip whatever she likes. I liked that apartment. It was home. I should've just stayed in it when you guys moved here."

"She will not thank you for this," Cam warned.

"Tell me something I don't know."

"I'll tell you something you don't know," Mavis hissed. "If you steal another cookie off this sheet to eat your feelings, I'm going to stab you with an icicle."

I looked down at the two small Christmas-tree-shaped cookies in my hands and smiled winsomely before shoving them in my mouth.

"Get out of my kitchen!" she yelled. "Both of you!"

"Yes, ma'am," I said around my ill-gotten sweets. "Love you, Mom."

She threw an oven mitt at my head as Cam started to bodily drag me to the living room. "Fucking annoying but lovable demons."

Once we were out of throwing range, Cam said, "Speaking of parents. Have you thought any more about the Penelope situation?"

"Can you be more specific?" I asked, hedging a bit. "I have many Penelope situations at the moment."

"Her parentage," he clarified.

I winced. I had been hoping they would give up on their mission to be the saintliest demons in Colorado until I had a chance to make Penelope love me again. Or, at the least, until she liked me again. I needed more time to make sure she would be safe if she ran off all half-cocked to find her asshole of a father. The demon's intricate world of brokering souls and bullying each other into whatever was the scheme du jour wasn't a place I wanted Penelope in. She was an innocent. She didn't realize her best friends, Cam and Mavis, were an exception to most demons. As demonic as they thought they were, they were different. They had consciences. They were raised to value life and be kind, just like Penny was. The majority of demons didn't value anything but themselves.

"Well?" he pressed.

"I have thought about it, Cam. You know I have. I just don't think right now is the time to spring that kind of news on her. She's already pissed at me. I don't want her pissed at you guys, too."

"I feel like a schmuck for keeping this from her for so long. She's not a kid anymore. We have to tell her soon."

"I don't want to lose her, Cam. Just give me a little more time."

Cam threw up his hands. "It's been more than seven months since she's spoken anything other than insults to you!" he hissed, glancing furtively in Mavis's direction. "Has it occurred to you that you may have already lost her?"

"Only every fucking day," I told him, my voice flat.

His face grew sympathetic as he calmed. "We have to do it soon, Rayonus. It's killing Mavis."

I sighed, hating that I had to keep secrets from my friends. I wanted so much to be able to tell him and Mavis the truth about my procrastination, to explain the reasons why telling Penelope would be a monumentally bad idea. But I just wasn't ready to expose myself because, as always in the case of demons, ignorance was definitely bliss.

Instead of doing the right thing and telling him all that, I said, "You know, Cameron, life was a lot easier when I had no morals. I was happy. I was carefree. I got laid. Wait. Why am I doing this again?"

"Because you love our fair Penelope," he said, clapping me on the back. "And you're not the half the jerk you used to be."

"Yeah, well, I wish I believed that."

Leaving Cam to his thoughts, I grabbed my jacket and stepped out into the cold October air, angry and desperate. The rage that had been building inside of me for the past year was a nearly tangible thing. I wanted out of this. I wanted a life—one without lies and deception.

But that was impossible and always would be. Because, though I might be walking around a free demon, in reality, I was caged—not by my secret assignment here in Havenwood Falls or the hierarchy of demons—by my fear, the fear that I would lose them all from my life if I told them the truth. They'd forgiven me after my first significant betrayal without any explanation. Another revelation could sever their faith in me forever. That was something I wasn't willing to risk.

CHAPTER 3

$\mathcal{T}$he next day, I arrived at Fairy Tale Florists early, hoping to learn as much as I could about the process before my first actual delivery. Finding the first floor empty, I climbed the stairs to find the second-floor offices much the same.

"Hello?" I called, listening for any noise.

"Rayonus? Is that you?" Rhiannon answered, climbing down from what must have been the turret. "I was just doing a little meditating. Are you ready to get started?"

I gave her an eager smile. "I am. What do we do first?"

"Follow me," she said, returning the smile.

It turned out there wasn't much to my job as a delivery driver. The names and addresses were checked and double-checked by a meticulous Reagan. The flowers were artfully arranged by the skillful hands of Rhiannon. It seemed my only tasks were loading the flowers into a specially designed van bearing the Fairy Tale Florists logo and driving them to various businesses and residences in the town tout de suite. I could do that. For Penelope, I could do any number of things.

The paperwork Reagan gave me a few short minutes of instruction later showed that my first delivery would take me straight to the source of all my stress. It was a hell of a way for the ladies to start me out, but one thing was for sure—every delivery after Penelope's would be a piece of cake. If I survived the interaction with all my appendages intact, that was.

After I loaded the massive arrangement into the van, I took a deep, steadying breath and drove straight to Havenwood Village. I knew Penelope would be home right now. She never went in to her job at Sakura Buffet before eleven. If my calculations were correct, she'd be smack in the middle of applying her makeup and trying to do something with her mass of beautiful long brunette curls right now.

I pulled into the parking lot a scant two minutes later and took another deep breath. And when I struggled to remove the vase from the contraption that kept it upright, I took another. Turning away from the flowers, I stared at her door. I had walked in and out of that door a hundred times, and during every one of those times, I had been the happiest I'd been in more than six centuries. Penelope was the most important thing in my life, and I would earn back her trust. Maybe it wouldn't be today or tomorrow, but it would come eventually. The weird relationship we'd fostered together was too important to both of us to stay like this forever.

In a better headspace, I turned my attention back to the task at hand and had to admit, while insanely huge and hard to manage, the roses and soft white flowers Rhiannon wove together with just the perfect amount of greenery were a thing of beauty. As soon as she told me orange roses indicated enthusiasm and passion, I knew there would be no other choice. I passionately and enthusiastically wanted Penelope back in my life. She had taken that sentiment to heart, creating an arrangement nothing short of a masterpiece.

Smiling wanly, I finally popped the vase loose and hefted the flowers onto one hip to knock on Penelope's door, waiting as patiently as one could for what was sure to be a disaster of epic proportions.

The door swung open almost immediately. "Hi! Oh, my gosh! They're stunning! Come in!"

I knew she would most likely react badly when she realized the identity of her delivery person, but I stepped in and took the chance, praying that this wouldn't be the last time she invited me into her apartment with that level of happiness.

"Just set them on the coffee table," she instructed, pure sunshine in her voice.

Fuck me; I didn't want to take that away from her. The absolute joy was like a balm to my aching soul.

Setting the flowers on the table, I had a mad urge to snatch the card from the holder before she saw it. This was too much. It was too soon. She wasn't ready to forgive me. What had I been thinking?

But it was too late. She'd plucked the card out of the middle before I had a chance to make my move.

"Thanks," she said, her eyes going from the tiny envelope to mine. "Ray."

I stiffened at the coldness in her voice but wanted to bask in her radiance like a housecat in the sun. Her hair was in a messy bun, and she had only lined one eye, but she was more beautiful than anything I'd ever seen. "Hello, Penelope."

Her gaze moved from my eyes to the logo on my chest. "You work for the florist now?"

I nodded. "I just started this morning. This is actually my very first delivery."

Her expression unreadable, she opened the envelope and pulled out the card.

"A secret admirer?" she asked, holding it out to show it to me.

"That is what it seems to say," I agreed, breathing an inward sigh of relief and thanking my lucky stars Rhiannon had the foresight to leave my name off the card.

She frowned. "Really, Ray. Are these from you?"

I shrugged and shook my head, hoping like hell that I looked innocent for once in my long life. "I'm afraid not."

Penelope knew me better than anyone else and probably didn't believe a word I was saying, but instead of fighting me on it as she was wont to do, she turned her attention to the flowers, stroking her index finger lightly over the delicate petals of a rose. "Thanks, Ray."

"It's my pleasure."

She didn't look up. "You need to go now."

"Of course," I said, giving her a ridiculous little bow that I would berate myself for later. "Have a good day at work."

Finally drawing her eyes away from the roses, she said, "You, too, Rayonus."

My name. She had used my name.

I beamed as I turned to leave. This felt like a win, and after the incident that had ruined things between us, I would take any progress I could get.

The incident . . .

What a colossal cock-up that had been.

Every time I thought about how close I'd come to losing everyone that meant anything to me, I wanted to sink into a deep, dark hole and wallow in my stupidity. But, at this point, so many months after, there was nothing I could do that hadn't already been done, no apology that hadn't been made. I'd made my bed with my choices, and it was time to stop hoping for Penny's forgiveness and start putting an actual plan into motion to gain that forgiveness. Nothing less would work with her, and I felt like an idiot for not realizing that from the start.

Moving back into the apartment I'd shared with Cameron and Mavis turned out to be much easier than I expected it to be. Partly because I chose a time in the early morning when I knew Penny would still be asleep, and partly because I was ecstatic to be so close to her, especially after what I was choosing to assume was an overture of civility the day before. I had practically hurtled everything I had to my name the short way to Havenwood Village with a genuine smile on my face.

Once I was done and sitting on the floor with my pitifully few belongings, though, I did feel a keen sense of loneliness, it wasn't something I was unused to; I'd always been alone before I came to stay in Havenwood Falls, but over the last year, I'd become so accustomed to Mavis's sarcastic and sometimes hurtful and painfully accurate quips and Cam's brotherly honesty and reprimands, I knew living on my own again would be an adjustment. They were, unequivocally, my family. Of course, family could be a giant pain in the ass, and I did have the comforting assurance that I could always visit Mavis for my daily abuse, so there was that.

Sighing, I picked myself up and shook off the feelings of dread and worry. I needed furniture and a lot of other little things that I should have taken care of a long time before I moved in. As much as I wanted it to, that kind of thing wasn't going to happen by itself.

Setting out on foot, I walked the short way to Room and dropped in on Melissa Lewis, where she helped me spend an exorbitant amount of money on things to make my living space homey. She assured me that was important, and I wasn't about to argue. After living with Mavis for so long, I knew better than to second-guess a woman who knew her stuff about decorating. After that, I made my way over to Callie's Consignments, where I spent an hour or so picking out furniture with Nikita, an unfamiliar death spirit. I arranged all of my purchases to be shipped to my apartment by CDI in a couple of days, though after I made the spur-of-the-moment decision to visit the human, Joshua, at Havenwood Falls Garage & Tow Service to buy the shiny silver pickup truck he had for sale, I had the means to move them myself. I figured the less time I spent traipsing in and out, the less chance of Penny imploding when she found out.

In the driver's seat of my new-to-me truck, I felt better, almost stronger. *I can do this,* I thought. I could live here full time in Havenwood Falls. It would be easy to become one of the fold. It would always be a little tainted by my secrets, but I could do this. For the chance to spend my life with Penny, I could do just about anything.

I showered and set up the TV on the bedroom floor after I returned to the apartment. Turning on a mindless sitcom, I rolled my puffy blue sleeping bag out on the carpet in front, stopping still, then landing heavily on my ass when the memory of the last time I'd used it —or hadn't used it—came barreling back.

It had been in the igloo, Mavis's wild idea of roughing it on the mountain in late March. Penelope and I had gotten drunk on Fireball and each other, both of us falling into her two-person sleeping bag to snuggle after Cam and Mavis went to "sleep." That had been the first time she'd kissed me, and it had met every expectation and desire I'd dreamed up inside my head. Her lips had been warm and soft, despite the cold. The taste of her? Cinnamon, whiskey, and Penelope. She had been a goddess that night, unabashedly telling me her secret fantasies and whispering things so dirty, I thought my brain would overheat from my desire for her.

I shook my head, ridding myself of the image of her flushed cheeks as she let go of her inhibitions that night. I couldn't dwell on what had been between us. Starting tomorrow, I was saying fuck it. Screw any fear I felt. I was starting fresh. Anything my friends asked, I would tell them. Anything they needed from me to prove myself trustworthy, I would give it to them. My decision had been made. After hundreds of years of lies, fake identities, and coercion, I wanted something real. The demon hierarchy be damned. They could find someone else to do my job.

CHAPTER 4

O n my way out to work the next morning, the first obstacle in
my grand plan hit me. Or rather, a hurricane of déjà vu hit
me as I walked out my door to see the same cross look on Penelope's
face that she wore the entirety of Mavis and Cam's beautiful gazebo
wedding in the square this summer. She had looked stunning in her
pale blue maid of honor dress, but it was that look that had nearly
stopped my heart. That look had haunted me and had distracted me so
thoroughly, I almost missed it when an amused-looking Addie
Beaumont dropped the f-bomb as she pronounced my favorite demon
couple husband and wife.

Arms crossed, which only served to compound that angry look,
Penelope asked, "Seriously?" bringing me out of my reverie.

Like a dumbass who had learned nothing from his past mistakes,
my first instinct was to feign ignorance. "Pardon?"

"Forget it," she said, angrily stomping back toward her door.

Lurching forward, I put a light hand on her shoulder to halt her
escape. "Wait a minute, Penelope."

She stopped but didn't face me. "What?"

The need to be honest with this young woman was a brute force
inside me, a constant banging in my head and heart telling me to do

the decent thing. It screamed at me to not be stupid this time, to tell the truth for once in my miserable life.

"I'm done lying to you," I said, finally finding my voice. "I want to earn your trust."

Turning suddenly, she poked my chest, her eyes ablaze with rage. "Bullshit."

"I'll tell you anything you want to know," I swore. "Anything."

Penelope stared at me. Then she hastily grabbed my hand to drag me into her apartment. "Come on."

Once the door was closed behind us and we were away from prying ears, she dropped my hand and whirled on me. "Why did you do it? Why did you kidnap me and set up Cam and Mavis to get captured last March? Just tell me the truth, Rayonus. I have to know."

I took a deep breath and began, more than ready to get this off my chest. "Ever since the day Severin brought Cameron to Havenwood Falls as a child, I've been tasked with keeping an eye on the activities of the cambions and other half-demons here. I am what the demons call a watcher."

A furrow creased her forehead. She had not been expecting that. "What?"

"There is a hierarchy within the demon ranks," I explained. "Those above me asked me to befriend demons who have children in Havenwood Falls to make sure they toe the line, and in return, they would forgive certain indiscretions of mine."

"So, you're like a spy?"

"A mole would be more accurate. I blend in, see what they're up to, then try to covertly stop them if they're using their younglings as weapons of mass destruction."

"That makes no sense," Penny said. "Weren't you Severin's evil henchman for like a hundred years?"

"Yes, and I'm not going to say aligning myself with Cameron's father didn't serve me well. Not all of what Severin got up to was world domination. We had our hands in a lot of pies and made a lot of money."

"So, what does that have to do with Severin's master plan to own Mavis and you kidnapping me to get her in his grasp?"

"Everything, really," I told her, taking a seat on her couch. "What I did was a means to an end. And as stupid, illogical, and hurtful as my plan was, it worked. Severin is dead, and you all are safe. I did what my assignment dictated me to do."

She sat next to me. "Do Cameron and Mavis know about this? About you?"

I shook my head. "I'm not supposed to tell the younglings or the parent, though sometimes it's unavoidable."

She pursed her lips. "So, you're telling me because it's unavoidable?"

"No, I'm telling you because I don't want to keep secrets from you anymore," I told her, risking rejection and a missing limb to cup her face in my hand. "I can't bear to hurt you more than I already have, and honestly, that angry, disappointed face you wear when you see me is making me feel . . . well, things—things I don't want to ever feel again."

Penelope stared at me, her face softening. "I want to trust you, Ray."

"Then trust me," I implored.

Shaking her head, she pulled away and stood. "How can I? You're basically telling me you're a glorified demon babysitter, which, by the way, makes you the absolute worst babysitter in the world. You almost got Cam and Mavis killed."

"Technically, Mavis was never in any danger. Severin would have roughed her up, but he wouldn't have done any permanent damage."

"Severin shot Cameron!" she exclaimed. "He could have died if he wasn't half-demon. And then you disappeared for two weeks after you brought me back to town. Where did you go? Didn't you care what happened to Cam and Mavis after we left them there with Cam's crazy-ass dad?"

I stood up and took her hand in mine. "Of course I cared, Penny. Who do you think cleaned that whole mess up? Do you think all of Severin's foot soldiers just disappeared after Mavis disintegrated him with her demon-killing power? Do you think they forgot she was the fabled Exitium Daemonium? Severin told everyone in his circle about her and his plan. I had to make sure they didn't come to Havenwood Falls for her themselves. Her safety —the safety of all of you—depended on them being taken out of the equation."

"I didn't think of that," she admitted.

"I didn't want you to think of it. And it would have been easier to tell you, but I wanted you guys to feel safe in your homes. I had already put you through enough to end that asshole's reign of terror."

She sighed. "If you just would've told us all this from the start, we could've stopped him some other way. We could have saved so much heartache."

"I couldn't tell you, Penny. Severin had a clairvoyant working for him." I pulled the ability-curbing amulet out of my shirt. "I was protected, but your minds would have been wide open to her."

"It's been seven months since all that. Why are you telling me now?"

I brushed a wild curl back from her face with my free hand. "I want you."

"Me?" she asked.

Lost in the beautiful brown of her solemn eyes, I said, "It can't be a secret, how much I care about you, how much I care about all of you."

"Then you need to tell Cam and Mavis. They deserve the truth."

"I'm pretty much an imposter, Penny. Do you really think Cam is going to be okay with me lying to him for a hundred years?"

Penelope threaded her fingers with mine. "You're not an imposter, Rayonus. You're his best guy friend. Friends forgive each other."

"Do you forgive me, Penelope? Are you my friend? I'm a demon. I do thoughtless, dangerous demon shit. Look how easy it was for me to lose you. Do you think he's going to overlook this right after I almost got him killed?"

She hesitated, biting her lip in thought before answering my questions. "Yes, I forgive you. And of course you're my friend. But it's going to take some time to trust you again fully. It will be the same for

Cam. Trust me; I know him much better than you do. He'll sulk and be pissed for a day, but then he'll come around."

Unable to stop myself, I pulled her into my arms and hugged her to my chest, reveling in her scent and the warmth of her body against mine. "I have an eternity. I can wait as long as it takes."

She grinned up at me. "Well, I don't have an eternity, so I don't think it will take quite that long."

"About that . . . ," I replied, only to be cut off by the ringing doorbell.

With an apologetic little smile, she pulled away and opened the door. Standing there were a grinning Cam and Mavis, both carrying takeout bags.

"We have breakfast burritos!" Mavis chirped, before her eyes fell on the unexpected demon in the room. "Ray? What are you doing here?"

While every part of me wanted to barrel through the couple and run far, far away, I knew that wasn't what was needed right now. It was time to come clean to the people I cared about. "Guys, we need to talk."

Wary, they both stepped into the apartment.

"What's going on?" Mavis asked, her eyes darting from me to Penelope.

I froze. How was I going to do this? I didn't even know where to start.

"Oh, for fuck's sake!" Penelope cried, throwing her hands up. "Ray is secretly some kind of super demon babysitter, and he's been assigned to Havenwood Falls by his demon bosses or whatever."

Cameron barked out a laugh. "Demon babysitter, huh? I don't recall you telling me any bedtime stories when I was a boy."

"It's true," I told him. "The hierarchy assigned Havenwood Falls to me when you were a toddler. There was an inordinate number of children that belonged to demons here at the time."

Stunned, Cameron sobered. "You're not kidding, are you?"

I blew out a heavy sigh. "No. I'm sorry I didn't tell you sooner. I should have, but it just got harder and harder as the years went on."

His voice ice-cold, he asked, "Because you were working with my father?"

"No!" I exclaimed. "I only worked with Severin because it was my job to know what your parents are up to."

"Our parents?" Mavis asked. "Ray, tell me you didn't know my grandfather was fake the whole time."

"I didn't," I swore. "I didn't know anything about you. I only found out you existed when Leon LeGrand came to Severin the day you ran away from him to ask him to use his clairvoyant to locate you. Utah wasn't in my jurisdiction."

"But you knew after?" Cam asked.

"Yes. And I did try to do what I could to help keep you both safe. Severin was so secretive about the whole Exitium Daemonium deal at the beginning. It was all I could do to keep one step ahead of them."

"One step ahead?" Cam growled. "My wife had to kill a pervert demon that broke into our apartment."

"Franco Ross was that demon," I supplied. "And the jerk was only there because I convinced Severin to send him in his stead to see what Mavis was capable of. She would have been taken if Severin came himself. He'd already had the Alchemist make an amulet to repel her magic. I made the only choice I had available to me." Turning my attention to Mavis, I said, "I'm really sorry you had to kill someone. That is not what I had hoped would happen."

"Apology accepted," Mavis replied, shrugging as she stood to start pacing the living room. "But I don't get it. Why didn't you tell us about this?"

Then she stopped, her mouth dropping open as the pieces clicked into place. "That was the woman who got in my head right before I killed Severin that day. That was his clairvoyant."

I nodded, relieved at the noticeable lack of anger in her voice, and pulled out the amulet around my neck again. "This is the only thing that saved my ass while I was there. It blocked her mindreading ability."

"I didn't know she could read my mind," Cam said, clearly thinking back to how much he'd unknowingly given away without even realizing it. "I just knew she was dangerous. How could I have been so careless?"

"Who would've guessed psychic?" I asked. "I was just lucky I had the amulet. Don't beat yourself up about it now that all that's behind us."

"Is it behind us, though?" Mavis asked.

"If you're asking if she's dead, then yes, I killed her. I killed them all. And I have no regrets for doing it. You guys' safety was and is my only concern."

Penelope sat on the couch and fished a breakfast burrito out of one of the bags, looking nonplussed. "Yeah, great. Everyone is dead. But let's back this thing up here." Taking a bite, she chewed for a moment, then asked, "If you didn't know about Mavis's parent, who are the other demon kids you referred to? You said, 'your parents' in the plural earlier."

Cameron and Mavis both gave me significant looks when I didn't answer Penelope's question right away. I returned it with a meaningful look of my own.

Alarmed, Penelope watched our game of facial charades for a moment, then her face crumpled. "Oh, fuck. It's me, isn't it?"

"Yes," we all answered in unison.

I added, "Only on your father's side. Your mother was human."

She rose, throwing the burrito on top of the paper bag. "Get out," she said, shooing us none too gently toward the door. "Now!"

Mavis sniffled. "We wanted to tell you, Penny. Please don't be mad."

Turning away from us once we reached the door, Penelope whispered, "Just go, Mavis. Just leave me alone."

Without another word, we did as she asked, though leaving her and hearing all the pain in her voice nearly broke me.

Outside, Cam stared at her closed door and asked, "What just happened?"

I checked my watch and sighed. "I happened, Cameron. I asked you not to tell her. If it's not perfectly clear, that's my demon gift. I fuck shit up. I destroy everything I fucking touch, and fuck me, it's fucked up timing, but duty is calling me in the form of a tasteful arrangement of posies due to be delivered to a human woman from a lovestruck werewolf. Apparently, time is of the fucking essence with these wolfy courtships."

Despite the shitty situation, the corners of Mavis's mouth quirked up. "That was an admirable number of fucks, Ray."

I smiled down at the petite little ice demon, surprised by her composure with the whole situation. "I can assure you. I meant every single one of them."

She returned my smile for only a moment, thinking better of it. "Dinner. Tonight at seven. Okay? Come prepared to talk. You've been excessively sneaky, and that ends tonight, or I'm putting you in timeout. Capisce?"

Hugging her to my side, I kissed the top of her head. "I'll be there, Mom." I held my hand out to Cameron. "Are we okay, Dad?"

After a second's hesitation, he shook it. "See you tonight, asshole."

Mavis rolled her eyes and looped her arm with her husband's. "Fucking annoying but lovable demons."

With one last look at Penelope's closed door, I saluted the two and ran for my truck, yelling, "Thanks, guys!"

CHAPTER 5

*A*fter my deliveries for the day were made, I didn't go home right away. Penelope was hurt, and if my history with her had taught me anything, it was that hurt eventually turned into seething hot anger. I would need to give her a wide berth for as long as I could. At the very least, until she stopped shooting the invisible laser beams of death out of her eyes.

Ducking into Howe's Herbal Shoppe, I took my time hand-picking bath bombs to be put in a fancily wrapped sage green gift box. Then I ran over to Sanguine Elixirs to get a bottle of the French champagne she liked. My plan was to get Penelope something I knew she'd love; something so lovely, it wouldn't end up in some weird science project on my doorstep the next day. Baths and booze were her two favorite things after the TV series *Supernatural* and pretty much every character from *Supernatural*. Except for Dick Roman, of course. Because, well, he was a dick, and she had season seven issues.

After splurging on the champagne and a couple of nice bottles of red wine for dinner, I took the things I'd bought for Penelope over to the OutPost Pack & Ship and had them carefully boxed together with a handwritten card I signed *from your secret admirer* in a moment of pure, unadulterated cowardice. I was not the proud, sardonic demon I usually was on this day. No. This was a new day, and on this day, I felt just as insecure as anyone else whose future relationships hung in the balance.

By the time I was done with my errands and back in my truck, I had just enough time to get to Cam and Mavis's house for dinner. With only a few moments to spare, I pulled into their driveway to find a frustrated Cam trying to unravel the various twinkle lights he was pulling out of a giant box. He looked absolutely miserable.

"Hey," I called, sliding out of the truck with the bottles of wine. "Need some help?"

"Yeah, go get two glasses and a corkscrew. No, fuck it. Just bring the corkscrew. We can drink out of the bottles."

"Things going that well out here, huh?"

He growled in frustration as he threw the twisted and tangled mess back into the box. "Why does she insist on reusing everything she found in the attic? These lights look like they saw their heyday in the eighties."

"Then this would be an excellent time to tell you about the multitude of brand new LEDs hidden in the garage?"

"Don't toy with me, Rayonus. I'm a man on the edge."

I laughed. "It's true. I had Blaekthorn Lumber and Supply call me as soon as they put them out on the shelf. I thought they might appease Buddy the Elf in there until we could get the actual trees."

Cam rolled his eyes in exasperation. "I ask you. Who decorates fake Christmas trees, then takes them all down to put up real ones? A year ago, she didn't even decorate. I don't know what's happened to her."

I shrugged. "We had a nice family moment, picking out that tree last year and decorating it."

"Hmph," he muttered. "Don't think I've forgotten that you also perpetuated Penelope's obsession with *Supernatural* with that nice family moment. Didn't we have enough of Castiel in our lives without looking at him on the top of the tree every day?"

"No," I retorted. "Because, unlike you, I'm not jealous of some fictional character. You know, just because Mavis had super-secret fantasies about doing it with Misha Collins, and you were too much of a horndog incubus to tell her no, doesn't mean you have to hate on Penelope's favorite character."

Disgusted, he said, "Ugh. You sound just like her."

I inclined my head. "I will take that as a compliment and hang on to it like a lifeline, thank you."

"You haven't heard from her, then?" he asked.

"Not at all, but I didn't really expect to. You?"

"Yeah, she called a couple of hours after we left and asked for more burritos to be left at her door."

I smirked. "Weren't there three burritos in each of those bags you left behind?"

Cam nodded. "Yes. Which is why she called an hour after the original burrito delivery with a request for ginger ale and Pepto Bismol."

"She's taking this to the extreme a bit, isn't she?"

"This *is* Penelope we're talking about," he reminded me. "It's your classic high drama, then sad, then angry, then over it scenario."

Grinning at the highly accurate description of my lady love's emotional process, I clapped him on the back. "Come on. We'll put this mess away after dinner and a few drinks."

He looked at the jumble of different styles of string lights and kicked the side of the box. "We're going to have to bury this thing like a body."

"Drinks first," I called from the porch. "Disposal of the Ghost of Christmas Past later."

Mavis had set a lovely tablescape for dinner—white candles, a pine cone and holly centerpiece, and actual crystal wine glasses to go with the delicate white gold detail of her wedding china. She was even using the gravy boat I bought to match—which, for her, was a bit disturbing.

"This is stunning, Mavis," I said, kissing her on her cheek and simultaneously taking the basket of what smelled like butter rolls covered in a white cloth napkin from her hands. "I would have changed out of my work clothes if I'd known we were having a fancy dinner."

"This isn't a fancy dinner," she corrected, pointing to where she wanted the bread placed. "It's a celebration. And I like seeing you in your work shirt. You don't look as shifty and useless as you usually do."

"Uh, thanks?"

"Don't mention it. Now give me that wine and go wash up for dinner. Our guest of honor will be here in a minute."

I groaned. "Please don't tell me it's Penny. You know she isn't past the initial shock. It will end badly."

"No, it won't," she insisted. "Because we're going to go out of our way to tell her all the good things about being a demon, and I'm going to get really, really drunk."

"There are good things about being a demon?" I asked, scrunching up my face. "Can you fill me in on some of the finer points before she gets here?"

She gave a martyred sigh. "Just go wash your hands before I put this meat fork to good use."

Grinning, I stepped out of her reach and blew her a kiss. "Am I going to have to call child protective services on you, Mom?"

"Either that or I'm going to end up smothering you with a pillow by the end of the night."

"Hey, that hits too close to home, Mavis. My mother did try to smother me with a pillow."

She gasped, horrified at her choice of words. "Oh, my gosh! I'm so sorry! I didn't mean anything by that!"

"I'm just kidding," I said, laughing as I walked to the sink. "She tried to drown me."

Narrowing her eyes, she shook her head. "I can't imagine why."

Penelope showed up only a few minutes after we popped the cork on the first wine bottle. Avoiding eye contact with me, she slid into her usual spot at the table and held out her glass.

"Are you sure drinking is a good idea, Penny?" Mavis asked,

hesitantly picking up the bottle. Clearly, she was having visions of a drunk demon crying on her shoulder all night.

"Yes, it's a good idea," Penelope snapped. "As a matter of fact, you drink your shit wine over there on the counter. I'll drink the two bottles Ray brought."

Puzzled, Cam asked, "How did you know Rayonus brought wine?"

"As I said, you buy shit wine. Ray is the only one with an eye for the good stuff."

"It's not so much the eye as it is the price. If it's over thirty-five bucks and foreign, it's a safe bet that it's a good bottle of wine."

She stared at me, her face shocked. "You are much less suave and debonair than I thought you were. Why am I not surprised?"

"Because I'm a demon?"

Penelope scoffed. "I'm a demon, too, and I'm refined as fuck."

"Without a doubt," I said, not about to engage with her while she was hovering between the angry and over-it stages of her demonic revelation.

"You may not be as urbane as I thought, but you can't deny that you're smart," she said, tipping her glass to me.

Smiling, I held her gaze. "I will take that as a compliment."

"And hang on to it like a lifeline?" Cam muttered under his breath.

I shot a glare at him as a too-bright Mavis jumped out of her seat and asked, "Who wants rolls?"

After a surprisingly explanation-free dinner and too many glasses of wine, Cam and I went in search of the LED lights to hang while Mavis and a pensive Penelope continued their boozefest in the living room. Because booze, plus demons, plus ladders were always a fine combination.

"Are you sure they're here?" Cam asked, looking in his fourth box to no avail.

Moving another box out of the way, I cursed. "They were here!

They were in a brown box with green and red print on the outside. I don't get it!"

"Wait," Cam said, spying the box on the opposite side of the room. "There they are." Wading through the piles of boxes we'd moved, he picked it up and shook it. "I know LEDs are lightweight, but this seems a little too light."

I sighed upon noticing that the box had been tampered with. "I don't think you want to open that box."

He furrowed his face. "Why?"

"Oh, just a hunch."

Setting the box down, Cam nudged it like there was a live snake hidden under the lid. "Hold me, Ray. I'm scared."

I snickered as I knelt to rip off the loose tape. Peering inside, I fell back on my ass, cackling with laughter. Inside was a note written in black Sharpie that read, *I TOLD YOU TO USE THE LIGHTS FROM THE ATTIC.*

"Mavis!" Cam yelled. "You suck!"

Immediately following this proclamation, we heard intoxicated giggles from the living room.

"Never get married," Cam warned. "It's all downhill after the wedding."

I shrugged. "If anything, that makes me want to get married more."

CHAPTER 6

*H*ours later, with the ancient lights detangled, hung, and lit, I went inside to say my goodbyes to the ladies. Both were sprawled out on the couch watching *Aquaman* for the hundredth time this year.

"I'm leaving. Penny, can I give you a ride home?"

Mavis sighed, staring at Jason Momoa's bare chest. "I know who I want to give me a ride."

"Then you should've thought of that while I still had my full incubus abilities," Cam said, scooping her off the couch. "You'll have to settle for riding me tonight."

She made a show of pouting, but mouthed, "Yay!" to Penelope and me.

We both shuddered.

"You know," Penelope slurred. "I think I will take that ride, Ray."

"I thought you might," I said, getting her coat from the rack in the foyer. "Night, guys."

There was no answer.

"Hurry," Penelope urged, nearly stumbling into me. "Before we hear something."

Laughing, I helped her over the threshold as she wobbled and steadied herself.

She broke away and skipped to the passenger side of my truck, all smiles and excitement.

"I like your truck," she said as I opened her door.

"Thank you," I told her, making sure her long flowy skirt was tucked into the truck.

When I rounded the hood and got in the driver's seat, she added, "I think this suits you."

"How is that?"

"It's big and manly like you. And it's shiny and pretty, but you know, not too pretty. It's basically you in truck form."

My smile was tight as I backed out of the driveway. "I'm not a man, Penelope. I'm a demon—a dumb-ass demon that makes huge mistakes and hurts the ones he loves."

"Nooooo," she whined, holding her hands out in the stop position. "I don't want to talk about that. Talk to me about something else. Like literally anything else."

I pursed my lips, trying to think of a safe topic, but all I could think about was how much I loved this woman and how fucking amazing she was. I finally settled on, "Well, I can talk about how downright delectable you look in that red top."

She traced a finger down the V-neck of her sweater to her cleavage and asked, "This red top?"

My cock punched up painfully in my jeans, reminding me just how long it had been since I had been able to touch her. I cleared my throat. "Yes, ma'am."

"Do you want to see what's underneath it?" she asked, toying with the bottom hem.

I didn't take the bait. Eyes straight ahead, I ignored the temptation and drove us as fast as I could down Eighth Street, swinging into my parking place less than a minute later. Without a word, I turned the engine off, jumped out of the truck, and ran around to open her door.

Penelope laughed at my theatrics. "Is that a yes?"

"That's a 'hell yes,' you beautiful, sexy woman. But it's also a little bit, 'I think you're too drunk to make good decisions, so I'm getting you out of the public eye before you get yourself arrested for public indecency.'"

"I like handcuffs," she mused, pressing her breasts against my chest as she slid her arms around my neck.

"So I've heard," I said, trying to coax her out of her seat.

She wrapped her long legs around my waist and nipped at my neck, biting hard enough I knew it would leave a mark. "I want you to handcuff me, Rayonus."

I gripped her ass and blew out a shaky breath as pure lust pulsed through my body. "I want to bend you over this seat, rip your skirt apart, and fuck you until you scream out my name."

When I pulled away to look at her face, I had to fight the need to do everything I'd just said. Her eyes were fiery, hungry, and all-consuming. She wanted that. She wanted me. But this was Havenwood Falls, not a porn set. Irene Beckett would be sure to walk by and have the whole town buzzing before church tomorrow if we so much as removed one shoe. It was risky enough just doing what we were doing.

"We'll talk about all the sexual fantasies you like once you're in your apartment," I bribed, lifting her up to carry her to her door.

"That's going to be hard, since I seem to have left my purse and keys on the coffee table," she purred, smiling like the cat that ate the canary. "Wherever will I sleep?"

I shut the truck door with a foot and laughed at the absurdity of the situation as I carried her koala-style to my apartment door. I had my hands on Penelope's perfect ass. Her legs were around my waist, putting her in a very favorable position against me. And if the nuzzles and nips to my jawline were any indication, she wanted to do a good portion of the filthy things she'd mentioned that night in the igloo.

The only problem was I was a fucking gentleman—gentledemon—whatever.

I groaned and leaned back away from her roaming lips, tongue, and teeth. "Penelope, as much as I'd like to give you that ride you asked for earlier, it can't happen tonight. When and if we ever fuck, I want you to be sober. I want to know you won't regret it, that you won't regret me."

Rolling her hips, she closed her eyes and breathed out a little contented sigh. "Trust me, Rayonus, regret is nowhere on my mind right now."

Hating what I was about to do, I eased her down to her feet and steadied her as she swayed slightly. "Penelope, I lied to you, put you in danger, and kept the biggest secret of your life from you. Tomorrow, when you're sober, you're going to remember that. You're going to remember all the pain and anger I've caused you."

I unlocked the door to reveal the empty apartment as she absorbed my words, all the while mentally bracing myself for her to revisit that anger, to strike out to hurt me as much as I hurt her, to give me the ass-kicking of an immortal lifetime, even. But she only cocked her head to the side and leered at the not-so-little problem in my work pants.

"I don't care," she said. "I want that."

I raised my brows and quickly shut the door behind us. "Say again?"

She bit her lip before speaking, but her eyes never strayed from the erection now throbbing in time to the beat of my heart. "I know I should care about all that. And I do. I'm drunk, not stupid. And I am mad. So, so fucking mad. And hurt. It took me so long to be able to trust you, and you fucked that sideways. But I realized something tonight at dinner."

"What's that?"

"I always held back when I thought I was human. I was scared of you—whether you'd be too much for me sexually or if you'd walk away once your overtly disturbing innuendos got you what you'd been after since we met."

I tensed as she spoke, my body taut with the need to show her who I truly was.

"What's changed?" I asked, closing my eyes and letting the façade I held onto for so long dissipate into nothing.

Penelope took an involuntary step back. "Rayonus, is this you? The real you?"

This was the real me, all right. I was showing her the form I hadn't seen for myself in decades. And I knew it might frighten her to see me as the black-eyed, seven-foot-tall, red-skinned demon I was born as. To human eyes, I looked like a thing of nightmares. But I needed her to see me as me, to see what was inside of me.

Reaching out, she touched the exposed skin at my collarbone, and I looked down, suddenly realizing that I'd ripped my shirt at the collar when I transformed.

"I'm sorry," I said, pulling off the shirt, then realizing I'd popped the button off my jeans. I held the shirt remnants low, covering myself.

She stared at me for a second, then did something wholly unexpected. She pounced on me, holding nothing back, knocking me to the floor and straddling me with her skirt bunched around her waist.

"What did you tell me you wanted to do earlier?" she asked, undulating her hips.

I spoke through clenched teeth as she brought all of my focus and resolve to a screeching halt.

"I want to bend you over," I said in a rough voice, fisting my clawed hand in her hair. "I want to rip your skirt apart," I continued, tearing open her red sweater to reveal a black lace bra.

She gasped as she moved against me. "And then what?"

Flipping her to her back, I growled, showing her my fangs as the heavy weight of my erection found her center. "I want to fuck you until you scream out my name."

Breathing heavily, we lunged for each other, both of us fighting for control in a clash of tongues, teeth, and fangs. Breaking away, I got to my knees and ripped my frayed pants open at the fly. A moment later, I was sheathed and ready for her. "Tell me to stop, Penelope."

She shook her head, slipping off her skirt and panties. Nearly naked, she rose to her knees in front of me, defiant as she met my tortured gaze. Her eyes were dark, fathomless, but her voice was as steady as stone as she smoothed her hand down the latex-covered length of me and said, "Never."

Every bit of restraint and self-control I had in me disappeared when I heard that word. In the fantasy I'd dreamed up over the past seven months, I'd pictured this moment to be a tender thing between us. I'd thought it would be slow, shy touches and languid kisses leading up to us making love.

Oh, how wrong I was.

This was rough. This was Penelope crashing her body into mine. It was me jerking her up to let her wrap her legs around my waist. It was her sex feeling like a blistering hot vise as she sank onto my cock. It was a year of wanting and need brought to an end.

"Fuck," she whispered, rolling her hips to grind against me. "Oh, fuck."

I stopped thinking. Hell, I stopped breathing. She was so impossibly beautiful with her lips parted, eyes closed in pleasure, and hair falling wildly around her. I wanted to own this demon woman. I wanted her to own me. I wanted us to be in each other's skin, for what we had together to be bone-deep within us, to be untouchable.

Grabbing her hips, I held her against me as I lay back on the carpet. She yelped in surprise at the sudden movement and opened her eyes to reveal the most predatory glare I'd ever seen on a lover. It was as if her hunger was consuming her from the inside out.

And that's when I noticed she had my amulet—the only thing that kept me together—wrapped around her hand.

CHAPTER 7

I woke to the unrelenting brightness of the sun in my face and a ringing in my head. Groaning, I rolled away from the window and opened my eyes, realizing the ringing was coming from the cell phone lying on the carpet next to me.

I picked it up and mumbled, "Hello?"

"What did you do?" a sly voice asked.

"We could be here all day with a vague question like that," I answered. "Want to narrow it down some?"

Mavis chuckled. "Oh, no. You know exactly what I'm talking about."

"No, I really don't. And honestly, I feel like I've been hit by a truck, so can we postpone this Q and A until later?"

"Rayonus, are you seriously not going to tell me how you managed to get Penny into your bed last night? Wait. Do you even have a bed yet?"

I sat up and dropped the phone, my hand going to the amulet that was, thankfully, back on my neck. Then my eyes widened in horror.

Penelope. Penelope had been here with me the night before. Frantic, I searched for the dropped phone and jammed it back to my ear. "What did she say? Is she okay?"

"Okay? Hmmm. Is she okay? Well, she moseyed all the way over here John Wayne style this morning because she couldn't walk right. I guess you could call that okay. And she's done nothing but sing the praises of your otherworldly demon dick every five seconds, so I'd say it's a pretty safe bet that you'll be getting a ten out of ten for your performance last night."

"I am relieved to hear it," I said truthfully.

"Then why do you sound like you've done something wrong?"

"That's the thing. She ripped off my amulet. I have no idea what I did."

She paused, and I could tell she was trying to decide whether or not she wanted to get involved. Finally, she said, "Explain, please."

"There's really not much to it. I'm chaotic without the amulet. I can go into a kind of frenzied state where I black out and, uh . . . do things."

"You lived with me a year, and you're just now deciding to tell me that's something that could happen?"

"You already knew that could happen, Mavis. Remember the igloo I took care of for you in March? No amulet, things get destroyed—that's the way it works."

"Well, I've seen what you 'destroyed' last night," she said, laughing at her joke. "And she's currently over here carb-loading French toast so she can make it through her work shift today. If you want to see her before she realizes what a terrible mistake she's made, now is the time."

"I can't this morning. I have furniture coming, but I'll stop by Sakura for lunch or dinner later to see her. Don't tell her I'm coming, okay?"

"Why?"

"Just don't. I want to see her reaction. She was buzzed last night."

"And you think that's why you got lucky? Oh, please. Penelope doesn't do anything she doesn't want to do. And I'm sure that includes you."

"I'm saying goodbye now, Mom."

She gave me a world-weary sigh. "Don't fuck this up, Ray.

I hung up the phone, looked down at what I'd just realized was my naked demon form, and prayed that I hadn't already fucked this up.

My new furniture started to arrive only moments after I'd showered and dressed for the day. As I assembled what little needed to be constructed, I tried to talk myself into going to Sakura Buffet for lunch. When I couldn't summon the courage for that, I moved the furniture around into different configurations and tried to talk myself into going there for dinner.

It was no use.

For the first time in my life, I was petrified. I didn't know what Penelope and I had done or even what we'd said to each other. There was no way I could possibly play this whole thing off. I was going to have to tell her the truth. But for someone like me, that wouldn't come easily. The truth bared a side of me that I'd kept hidden for excellent reasons.

But by four thirty, I realized I had moved the couch eight times and had to slap myself mentally. I couldn't fight the urge to see her anymore. I was driving myself crazy.

Jumping into my truck, I drove to Miller's Plaza as fast as the law allowed, hopping out as soon as I shifted it into park. Since it was relatively early for dinner, there were only four people inside the restaurant—Penelope, looking like a fucking goddess in her uniform; Dao Pham, the darkly seductive and well-dressed female owner that I hoped I never had the misfortune of running afoul of; Mavis, who was smirking at me like it was her job; and Dade, the guy from Hey, Nice Glass! who shone like a beacon to the soul-sucking demons in town, but didn't really seem to stand out to the humans in his almost constant attire of novelty T-shirts and jeans. Every one of them looked up from what they were doing when I walked in.

Silently cursing the fear I felt as I approached the counter, I smiled sweetly at Penelope. "Can I get a to-go plate and the license plate number of the truck that ran over me last night?"

The corner of her mouth quirked up as she punched the order into the register and took my money. "Hey, you aren't the one whose sore thighs were making her waddle around like a duck this morning."

"No." I reached up to stroke the tiny white flowers she'd woven in her braid. They were from the arrangement I'd given her. "But I was the one who was left to wake up alone, wondering where you'd gone off to."

"Well, you won't have to wonder where I'm at tonight. I'm coming to your place when I get off."

I lifted a brow at her choice of words and leaned in close, unable to let an opportunity for sexual innuendo pass by me unchecked. "Penelope, I cannot wait for you to get off."

Pink-cheeked and smiling, she handed me a container for my food. "See you shortly after ten."

"Yes, you will."

Mavis and Dade were both smirking at me when I turned around. I narrowed my eyes at Dade, expecting him to look away, but he merely grinned, speared a piece of sweet and sour chicken, and popped it in his mouth with a sarcastic little fork salute.

"Dude, do you know how long I've been waiting?" Mavis asked, drawing my attention away from the odd young man.

I gave her a perplexed look and filled my plate before I sat down across from her. "Want to fill me in on why you're waiting for me, weirdo stalker?"

She pursed her lips like she had been sucking on something sour. "I didn't think you'd show up is all. I might have made a wager on whether or not you'd show."

It was my turn to smirk. "I told you I would be here. Why would I not show up?"

She gave me a droll look. "You know exactly why, Ray."

I shook my head and stood. "You need a hobby, Mavis."

"Your guys' relationship drama over the past seven months has been my hobby," she hissed. "I'm invested now. It's like witnessing a real-life soap opera. You can't take that away from me."

"I'm telling Cameron," I told her, picking up my plate to leave. "You need an intervention."

"I can quit anytime I want!" she yelled at my back.

Dao looked up from where she was counting the till and cut her eyes at me. I shrugged apologetically at the distinctly nonhuman woman and picked up the pace. Even to a demon, Dao Pham was more than a little scary.

CHAPTER 8

$\mathcal{P}$enelope didn't show up as promised after she got off from work. Instead, she texted.

COME OVER AS SOON AS YOU GET THIS!!!

I frowned as I read the text. I didn't know why, but those words were screaming, "There's something terribly wrong that's going to disrupt our already precariously balanced lives" to me.

"This is going to be bad," I groaned, grabbing my coat.

There was no answer at her door when I knocked. No sounds or noises either.

I sighed, not knowing what to expect as I fished out the key she'd given me many months before and stuck it in the lock. Stepping in, I shed my coat and closed the door behind me. "Penny?"

"Ray?"

I held a hand to my chest when my initial panic eased a bit. She was coherent. That was always good.

"Where are you?" I called.

"The bathroom. Can you come here, please?"

In the back of my mind, I knew that what I was about to see wasn't going to be one of those "Dear Penthouse" scenarios, but I certainly didn't expect to see what I saw.

"Holy shit," I said, taking in everything.

"That's all you have to say?" she asked, throwing her loofah at me.

I stared down at the naked demon sitting in the bath. "I'm trying to decide what I'd like to talk about first."

"Oh, I don't know. How about the fact that I'm a demon?"

I sat down on the edge of the tub. "Yeah, but you were already a demon. I think you naked in this bathtub might be the bigger story here."

She slapped the bathwater to get my attention. "You know what I mean!"

I did know what she meant. But fuck me, she was so stunningly beautiful right now; I couldn't stop gawking at her. I shook my head as I reverently looked over the amazing transformation of her body. Her body was always long and lean, but now her skin was bronzed, her frame more muscled, and there were new angles on her face, each as sharp and defined as the fangs in her mouth and the claws on her fingertips. "Penelope, you have no idea how beautiful you are to me right now."

Her breath quivered. "And you have no idea how much I am freaking the fuck out."

I cupped her cheek. "Tell me how I can help, demon lady."

She glared at me, but said, "I need three things from you."

"Please tell me one of them is my seed," I pleaded. "Because damn." I frowned, suddenly remembering who I was talking to. "Oh, wait. This isn't going to be some kind of riddle, is it? Or a quest?"

"Stop trying to make me laugh," she said, poking out her bottom lip, which was a little harder with her shiny new fangs.

"What will you have me do, milady?" I asked, grinning as I leaned in to kiss her pouty lips.

"First, you're going to tell me whether or not you're my secret admirer," she said, giving me a hard stare. "The next two things will depend on that answer."

"Yes, I am your secret admirer," I admitted. "Are you surprised? You didn't think it was Dade, did you?"

"What?" she asked. "Who?"

I waved the thought away. "Never mind. What are the other two things?"

"Can you get me the champagne and bath bombs you sent from the table?" she asked meekly, batting her eyes.

I sighed and jumped up to do her bidding. "Do you need a glass or are you going to just drink out of the bottle like you normally do?"

She groaned in annoyance. "Shut up and go get it."

Closing the door behind me, I leaned my forehead against the wall and sighed in relief. Since we'd apparently had more sex than the Kama Sutra had positions, I shouldn't have been so shocked by her complete nudity, but I was. I was a six-hundred-year-old demon who was acting like I'd just seen my first naked lady.

"Get yourself together," I whispered, pushing away from the wall and running to grab what she'd requested. She needed more from me than my dick right now.

When I came back in, she was rewarming the water and looking a little more chipper. Handing her the box of bath bombs, I set her glass on the edge of the tub and popped the cork out of the bottle.

"Are we going for taste or speed of drunkenness?" I asked, pouring a bit into the glass.

"Speed," she said. "And I'm kind of sad that you had to ask me that."

"Not at all." I filled the glass up to the top and handed it to her. "Here you go, lushie."

Still a little shaky looking, she hugged her knees with one arm and took a sip out of the glass with the other. "Thanks."

I took a swig of the warm champagne and gagged. "I know it's been a hard night for you, but how the hell are you drinking this warm?"

"Trust me. After what I've seen today, it's easy," she said, dropping a fizzing orb into the water then downing the contents of her glass. "Really, really easy."

I gave her a refill and gestured to her naked body. "Are we talking about seeing more than the extreme sexiness you've got going on right here?"

She nodded. "I'm talking about my boss having six tails. I'm talking about the werewolf that came in for a late dinner just before closing. I'm talking about the red-skinned demon I'm looking at right now."

I stared at her for a second, then jumped up to look at myself in the foggy mirror. Nope, no red-skinned demon, just the façade I wore while I was around others. "Penny, how do you see my form while I'm not wearing it?" I held out a hand. "No, wait. Dao has six tails?"

She choked back a laughing sob. "I don't know how I see it. I've always been able to tell when people weren't quite human. It was a gift I didn't want but couldn't get rid of. But this—this is the gift on steroids. I can see everyone's forms flickering around them as if they're almost but not quite tuned in. And to top all that off, I can't figure out how to make my human form come back out."

"Man, Cameron is going to be pissed when he sees you're able to shift forms. Most half-demons can't."

"Not really my concern right now," she deadpanned.

I laughed. "I know, but there's not much you can do about it that you haven't already done. You've already gotten the tattoo from the court, so there's no worry about the humans."

Her mouth dropped open. "I have a tattoo?"

"Yes." I pointed to the invisible ink on her shoulder. "It was done when you were first placed here in the Falls. Otherwise, this may have happened while you were in school or somewhere else in public. Can't have you demoning out at recess."

"Not that I'm complaining or anything, but we really should have talked more last night. There's still so much I don't know."

"About that," I began.

She held her hands up in the stop position. "Nope. I don't want to know."

I gave her a sheepish look. "But you need to know."

"Damn it!" she growled. "Isn't my day going bad enough?"

"Yes? No? I honestly don't know how to answer that, Penelope."

She glared at me, held up a finger, then downed her glass. When I refilled it with the rest of the bottle, she said, "Get naked. There's enough room for both of us in this tub."

"Do you really think us both being naked will improve the situation?"

"Get. Naked," she reiterated.

"Okay, but once I'm naked, I get to come clean about everything. No pun intended."

She grinned excitedly and bounced up and down, which didn't do anything to help me in the staring department. "Deal."

With a reluctant groan, I kicked off my boots and socks and stood to take off my shirt, jeans, and underwear. Getting certain sensitive body parts close to her when I was about to tell her things she didn't want to know was probably the worst plan ever. But it was apparent Penelope thought the opposite. She never stopped watching me as I undressed. Her face never lost that stunned, amazed expression, as if she couldn't believe what she was seeing.

That expression did not suck for my ego.

I kicked my clothes into a little pile and stood up straight in front of her. "Do you like what you see?"

She leveled a stare at me. "Do I like what I see? Are you kidding? Fuck, yes, I like what I see. If I weren't so sore from last night, I would climb you like a fucking tree."

"Good to know," I said, easing into the hot water behind her.

Settling in between my legs, she laid her back against my chest and sighed as I cupped her breasts.

"That didn't take long," she said, laughing.

"Sorry, it's instinctual to me, like breathing."

"And the erection against my back?"

I kissed her temple. "Same goes."

She closed her eyes, relaxing against me. "I'm glad you're here right now. You're a nice distraction."

"I've been called worse."

"I'll bet you have. What do you think I'll call you when you 'come clean'?"

"Hmmm . . . honest? One would hope, anyway."

"Not something I would normally expect out of you," she said. "But you do seem to be trying it out lately. Okay. Shoot. Be honest with me."

"Okay." I blew a long slow breath out of my nose. "When I woke up this morning, I couldn't remember most of last night."

She turned in my arms to look up at me. "What parts of last night?"

"Every part after you took off my amulet."

Her forehead wrinkled in confusion. "What do you mean?"

I sighed and lifted the amulet to look at it before dropping it back down against my chest. "Having this thing is a double-edged sword. It protects me and diminishes my abilities to keep me from making catastrophic mistakes, which is great, but because I've become so used to having my power dampened, it's really easy for me to slip into a kind of frenzied state when it's off. During those times, I can't remember much of what I do."

"What do you remember from last night?"

"You looking like you were about to fuck my brains out with my amulet wrapped around your wrist."

She looked horrified. "I'm sorry, Rayonus. I guess I just ripped it off in the heat of the moment. I don't even remember doing that."

"No, I'm sorry. If I was honest with you like I should have been, you would've known that was a possibility."

"So, we can just agree we're both sorry and leave it at that?" she asked hopefully.

I laughed. "No freakin' way. I want to know what you did to me while I was out of it. Anything kinky?"

"You mean, what you did to me," she retorted. "I didn't get a chance to do anything."

I cringed. "That does not sound good."

"Good doesn't even come close to it, Ray. You were an animal for three straight hours. And I don't speak Renaissance-era Latin, but you do, and I was pretty into whatever you were saying. It all sounded like an orgasm for the ears, and by the end of the night, an orgasm for every other part of me."

Trying hard to tamp down the smug smile spreading across my face, I asked, "Do you remember anything I said?"

"Yes. You kept whispering *te amo* into my neck and something that sounds like *uxor mea.*"

"I love you, my wife."

She smiled. "That's what you were saying?"

"*Omnia mihi es,*" I told her. "You are my everything."

"I'm not going to lie. You were pretty focused last night. I felt like I was your everything. I just wish you could remember it."

I wrapped my arms around her stomach. "Honestly, I'm just thankful I didn't bring the building down on top of us. Usually, when the necklace comes off, bad things happen—bad things like property damage and demon murder."

She laughed. "You did shake the room for a brief second, but it wasn't bad enough to do damage. You tried to be as gentle as you could through it all."

"So, I didn't hurt you?"

"Only in very good ways—a light bite on my neck, the tips of your claws digging into my ass—the only thing that's still sore is my well-used . . ."

"Okay," I said, interrupting her. "That's enough of that talk."

She laughed. "I'm just saying, A plus for effort. And also for skill. You pretty much ruined me for all other demons."

I lifted the heavy weight of her hair away from her neck and scraped my fangs across the delicate wet skin. "Good, because I don't plan on letting any other demons have you—ever. I want you as my mate."

CHAPTER 9

With a much calmer and drier Penny fast asleep in her bed, I made a phone call I hoped I would never have to make.

The Alchemist answered after only one ring. "Rayonus Rixa. I haven't heard from you in almost a year."

"Yeah, well, I've been busy," I told him.

"With my little girl?"

"She not a child anymore, Draz, as you well know," I said. "She's almost twenty-four."

"Even so, you know it's frowned upon for someone in your capacity to fraternize with our younglings."

"I do. Just like I know it's frowned upon to fraternize with their parents. But I'm calling you for a reason."

"And that is?"

"I need an amulet made."

He sighed. "Not for you, I hope? Your amulet wiped my magic out for a week after I made it."

"No, not for me. Do you really think I'd be coherent enough to make a phone call without my protection?"

"No, I suppose not. But you do know I don't make these things for just anyone. I would need to deem them worthy, and they must align themselves with me in the event I should ever need their power."

"No."

Draz chuckled. "Those are and have always been my terms."

"Not with me and not with the owner of this amulet. She needs it, and you will give it without expectation, just as you did for me."

"It's for Penelope, isn't it? She has my power."

The way he said "my power" made my skin crawl. "It's nothing that could help you," I told him. "She only sees the creature underneath. She can't seal their powers away like you can."

"Not yet, she can't. But it will only take a few lessons."

My voice unwavering, I said, "We're not doing that again. You tried that, remember? With your son. The one that had to be killed when you pushed him to the brink of insanity."

"Think of it as trial and error," he said, dismissing my reminder of his all-too-recent failure.

"I'll think of them as your younglings, Draz. You only have one left. Do not attempt to sway her to do your dirty deeds. If you hurt her—if you so much as lay a finger on her—I will be the end of you. Testor ego eam."

After a long pause, he finally said, "Bring her to my shop in Patriam tomorrow evening. I will make the stone, and I will not mention our relation. But after this, I will ask that you will cease to watch over my child."

"Do as you must," I said, not giving a tin shit what he wanted. Penelope was mine to protect whether it was my assignment or not. She was going to be my mate. The demon in me—in both of us—had chosen.

I hung up with Draz and peeked in the bedroom door at Penelope. Back in her human form, she looked peaceful and content as she slept —all the worry and fear she'd felt just a few minutes earlier absent from her mind.

Frowning, I silently stepped into the room and sat on the foot of the bed. I wanted to just live in that quiet moment and keep her away from all of the demon bullshit she was about to be immersed in. It was for the best that she knew what her father was capable of, I knew, but that didn't mean I had to like it.

Shifting slightly, she opened her eyes and smiled at me. "You look worried. That's becoming a thing with you."

"I'm not worried at all," I lied, stretching out beside her and pulling her into my arms. "But I am thinking about taking you someplace tonight. Can you get off from work?"

She nodded against my bare chest. "I'm already off tonight. Where are we going?"

I sighed. "To what we demons call Patriam."

She propped herself up on an elbow. "Patriam? Like, in the demon underground? But didn't Cameron say that place was dangerous?"

"For him, yes. It's quite dangerous. He's half-human."

"I'm half-human," she reminded me.

I tucked her hair behind her ear and pulled her back into my embrace. "You'll be with me, love. And we aren't going to hang around long enough for anything to get dangerous. We're going to see the demon we call the Alchemist and then we're going home. He's willing to make you an amulet to seal your power away."

"Oh, thank God," she said, relief coloring her voice.

"But, before we go to all the trouble of going there and having to deal with some inevitable demon-related shit, I will say that I think you could perform that magic yourself without exposing yourself to the others, especially one as dangerous to you as the Alchemist."

"How do you know?"

I pressed my lips together. "Because you undoubtedly have similar powers to your father. That's the way it always is."

"Still, shouldn't we err on the side of caution and get the amulet anyway, just in case things take an unexpected turn?"

"I'm not sure seeing the Alchemist would be considered erring on the side of caution. Seeing him puts you in much more danger."

"Why?"

I rolled onto my back, taking her with me. "Because he wants to own you, just like he's wanted to own all of his children."

Her brows furrowed as she looked up at me. "Are you trying to tell me my father is the Alchemist?"

I closed my eyes and nodded. "That is what I'm saying."

"And you've known this for how long?"

Sensing the storm of her anger rumbling in the distance, I cracked an eye open. "Around a quarter of a century."

"So, my entire life, basically."

"Basically."

She groaned and flopped her head onto my chest. "Why do you tell me things I don't want to know, Ray?"

"Because you get violent when I don't tell you and your fists of fury hurt . . . a lot."

"Stop bringing logic into this conversation. You know that's not the way you do things."

I laughed. "Have you ever thought that maybe that's why I always get the demons I love into bad situations? I think logic *should* be brought into our conversations."

"Pssshh . . . where's your sense of adventure?"

CHAPTER 10

The trip we took to Patriam was the work of a moment. One second we were standing in my living room, dressed and ready to leave, and the next, an amazed Penelope and I were standing in the weakening evening sun on a nearly empty street, just outside the entrance of the demon settlement.

She narrowed her eyes at me. "Next time, warn a girl! I didn't even know you could do that!"

I shrugged, checking around us to make sure no one had overheard her human decree. "There's a lot about me you don't know," I said, wrapping an arm around her shoulders. "I plan on giving you little tidbits of information over the next two hundred years or so to keep you guessing."

She stared at me. "You are so fucking weird at the oddest of times, Rayonus."

I kissed her forehead. "You using my real name negates the insult. Just so you know."

"I think you're immune to my insults anyhow," she said, turning toward what appeared to be a group of black-shawled demons heading our way. "Friends of yours?"

"Scavengers," I told her, leading her down a path in the direction of the town. "Best to avoid them."

"Noted." She glanced behind us. "Anything else I need to worry about?"

I grinned, enjoying myself a little more than I probably should have. "Do you want me to put it into some pop culture references you might understand?

"Do you really have to ask?" she retorted.

"Okay. Where we're going is like Diagon Alley. It's full of interesting demons and magic. Where we are now is like Knockturn Alley. Here, you don't want to stray from the path. If you do, don't let anyone try to show you the way back. And whatever you do, don't make eye contact. Just stay near me and try not to get separated or buy any owls . . . or magic wands . . . or books that try to eat you."

She smirked. "So, keep my half-blood ass in line and let you eat me?"

I pressed a kiss to her hand and led her into the dozens of demons milling about the stands and stores on the street. "You do have a way with words, my love."

"I can't believe you said that instead of coming up with some kind of sexual innuendo about oral sex," she said, looking up to me as I led her through the crowd of increasingly inquisitive demons. Either she was so cool that she hadn't noticed their stares and whispers, or she was willfully ignoring them to show no fear. Either way, she was killing it. Nothing was more respected in this town than a demon who had balls, so to speak.

Meeting her halfway, I kissed her lightly, then captured her bottom lip between my teeth and bit down ever so slightly, just hard enough to make her gasp and pull me closer. "I will talk to you about oral sex as much as you want, once we've completed our business here," I whispered against her mouth. "Count on it."

Her lips quirked up into a smile. "Trust me, Rayonus. I will."

I met several greedy eyes when Penny and I separated and continued walking. I gave every last one of them a look that said in no uncertain terms that the demon in my arms was my mate, that I had claimed her, and that she wasn't up for grabs. One by one, they turned away, showing defeat. No one wanted to fuck with the watcher. Stories of the demon before the Alchemist helped me restrain my power still circulated around the fires. I was too wild, my magic unpredictable. I was to be feared.

And I was . . . for the most part.

There would always be someone out there who wanted the recognition, the glory, of defeating the undefeatable. Those demons, I let be. But that's not to say I didn't keep an eye on them.

"Where is this place?" Penelope asked. "None of the stores have signs."

"That's because these stores cater to people who live here. Outsiders aren't usually welcome."

"Sounds quaint. When can I expect to be murdered by a local?"

I shook my head. "As long as you're with me, never."

She threaded her fingers with mine. "Then consider us joined at the hip."

"You just can't stop yourself from giving my dirty mind openings like that, can you?"

She shrugged. "It's more like I don't want to."

Laughing, I wove us around the crowd and down to the narrow alleyway that led to the Alchemist's home. "Here we are."

Penelope eyed the worn door and the surrounding dirty walls. "This is where I could have grown up?"

"Not what you were expecting?" I asked.

She shook her head. "Not even close."

"Oh, it wasn't too bad, growing up in Patriam. There are much, much worse places to live in our little demon underworld. Ones I hope to never have to show you."

"I will do everything I told you I wanted to do in the igloo if you never show them to me," she said, fighting a shiver.

"Deal," I told her, reaching to knock on the door. "Ready?"

"As I'll ever be."

I'd warned Penelope earlier that Draz said he would keep their relation a secret and that she was under no obligation to mention she knew the truth, but somehow, even before the door swung open, I knew she'd blow that whole thing wide open. That was Penelope's style —shock and awe.

"'Sup, Dad," she said, stepping in the doorway before he could invite us in.

I bit my lip to keep from laughing at Draz's stunned face. I was guessing he was in his demon form to try to intimidate her, but his wasn't much different than her own, and compared to mine, it wasn't even remotely terrifying. If anything, it probably pissed her off more.

"Hello, daughter," he said in return. "How do you fare this evening?"

Rolling her eyes, she said, "Cut the shit, Draz. I need the amulet. Give it to me, or I'll make one for myself."

Looking to me for an explanation, Draz held up his clawed hands in a *what gives* position.

I shrugged. "Draz, meet your daughter, Penelope, and her wildly inappropriate temper."

Not sure whether I was joking, he smiled at her, fangs on full display. "It's nice to meet you, Penelope.

"Is it?" she asked, staring him down.

He shot another dumbfounded look my way.

I stepped between them, hoping to defuse the situation. "Okay, I can see this is going nowhere fast. Draz, we've come for an amulet for your daughter. Will you make it for her, or is she going to have to shove her size nines up your ass?"

He turned an overexaggerated bright smile on his offspring. "Of course! I'd be happy to help her! Just leave it to us, and I'll have her ready and back on the road to Havenwood Falls in a jiffy."

Did he just say *a jiffy*? I narrowed my eyes at him. "I'm not leaving her alone with you."

Clenching his jaw for a moment to get his temper under control, he spat, "I told you, Rayonus, you aren't to watch her anymore. She's my daughter. I will request another watcher, one who hasn't become enmeshed in the lives of his wards. You have no rights to her."

Alarm bells went off in my head. Draz was usually civil with me, though it was more likely that he was afraid of me than because of a mutual respect. After all, he alone knew how powerful I was. If he was choosing to stand up to me like this now after centuries of near-cowering, something important was in the works. Something he didn't want me to impede.

"Rights or not, Rayonus does whatever he wishes to me," Penelope purred, tangling her hand in mine and throwing gasoline on an already out-of-control flame. Clearly, she wasn't used to dealing with demon politics.

"You dare to defile my daughter without my permission?" Draz shouted.

Penelope smiled frostily at the angry demon. "Like you even care. Make the amulet, Draz. Or don't make the amulet. I don't give a shit. But I'm tired of you wasting our time."

Draz's shrewd, calculating eyes roamed from me to his daughter. "I have no problem making it for you, daughter, but I will not give our secrets to him. You may have them, but he will not. He will use what little power we've gained against weaker demons. Surely, you can sense how powerful and dangerous he is."

"He stays," she said plainly, her voice almost bored.

"Then, I'm sorry, Penelope. I cannot make the amulet."

Penelope turned on her heel and walked to the open door. "See ya, pops."

"It appears we will not be needing your services," I said, following her to the door. "Until next time."

"Don't either of you dare darken my doorstep again!" he screamed after us.

I turned and raised an eyebrow at this unusual display of anger, but Penelope just continued walking, her middle finger held up high as she went.

When the noise of Draz's roars were shut off by the closing door, Penelope hurried back to me and looped her arm in mine. "I might have gotten a little carried away there. I almost forgot where I was."

"I'd say you got just enough carried away."

"How so?"

"Well, any less and Draz might have noticed that we took his book with the instructions for your amulet." I patted my pocket. "Did I mention that I have excellent sleight-of-hand abilities?"

She grinned up at me as we quickly made our way down the street. "You did not. Am I to assume that's one of the tidbits you mentioned that you'd be sharing over the next two hundred years?"

"You are. Impressed?"

"Very. But how do you intend to play it off once he realizes it's gone?"

I stopped at a secluded ivy-covered staircase and led her down. Unlocking the hidden door, I pulled the chain of an old lamp to illuminate the small but clean parlor and locked the door behind us.

"He won't realize it's gone," I told her, taking out my camera to snap pictures of the pertinent information. "We're going to take these pictures, and then I'm going to return it using teleportation. Even if he already knows it's gone, he'll just think he overlooked it when he finds it. But chances are, he's so mad, he won't even think to look for it."

Her eyes were wide as she stared at me. "You're some kind of evil genius, aren't you?"

I chuckled. "Not what you expected in a mate?"

Her brows furrowed. "Yeah, about that. What is all this mate stuff?"

"It just means I've chosen to mate with you. If you're willing to accept me," I added lamely.

"Mate? As in a sexual partner?"

I nodded. "Sort of, yes. Demons aren't really into the whole monogamous thing; they usually just fuck anyone—human, demon, or other—no strings attached. Mates stay together. Sometimes not forever, but generally, for a few decades or centuries."

"So you were serious about that Latin wife stuff the other night?"

"I can't be anything else without my amulet. When it's off, you get the real me."

"I like the real you," she said, putting her arms around my waist. "He's hot."

"Hold that thought," I told her, disappearing for a split second to slip the book back into Draz's home.

When I returned, she smacked my shoulder. "Stop doing that!" she exclaimed. "I don't know where I am!"

"You're in my home," I told her, rubbing my shoulder. "Did you really think I'd leave you somewhere where you could have been in danger?"

Her interest piqued, she glanced around the parlor. "This is really your home?"

I watched her as she took in the paintings in gilded frames on the wall and the vintage furniture from decades past. "My home when I'm in Patriam, yes."

"What's back here?" she asked, pointing at the closed door that led to the rest of the house. "Dungeon? Demon torture chamber?"

"I hate to disappoint, but that's the hallway leading to the kitchen, bathroom, and my bedroom."

Brows raised, she walked to the door. "May I?"

"Feel free to roam wherever you'd like. We have time. According to Draz's book, we have to gather a few materials before you can make the amulet anyway."

She nodded and stepped to the door, hesitating for a second before she reached for the knob. "Is there anything dangerous back here?"

"There might be some twenty-year-old Pop Tarts in the kitchen. I'd stay away from those."

She shook her head with an expression of exasperated humor on her face. "There's something really wrong with you."

Laughing, I swung the door open to the darkened hallway and flipped on the lights. "You're not the first to say it."

"That does not surprise me," she said, stopping in front of the door at the end of the hall. "Bedroom?"

I nodded, wondering what she'd think about the ridiculously ornate demon-sized bed within.

"Wow," she said, marveling at the room when I turned on the lights. "This is your bedroom? It looks like a gigantic king lives here."

"Not a king, just a giant demon."

"Is this where you lived before you moved in with Mavis and Cameron?"

"Yes. I still live here off and on, though I haven't been here for a month or so. I just come back every so often to dust and change the sheets. I like to keep it ready and maintained in case my situation ever changes, and I have to return."

To my surprise, she kicked off her sneakers and ran to the bed to dive on top of the duvet. "I love it," she said, stretching out her arms. "We could sleep together and never see each other in this thing."

I unlaced my boots and climbed onto the bed after her. "I don't care what bed we're in. We will be seeing each other in it. And hopefully, you'll be naked."

She laughed sultrily as I grabbed her leg and yanked her under me. "Naked in human form or demon?"

I feigned thought. "You know, when it comes to us having sex, I don't think I have a preferred form. I'd be delighted to take you any way I can."

"I've never had sex as a demon," she reminded me, unbuttoning her shirt and unclasping the front clip of her bra to expose her breasts. "Is it any different?"

"I'm not sure," I said, getting to my knees to pull my shirt over my head. "Think we should give it a try?"

"For research purposes?" she asked, reaching down to unbutton my jeans.

I closed my hands over hers to stall the hurried movements she was making and stood to shed my clothes. If she continued like this, I would burst out of them Hulk-style and have to dig through my closet in hopes of finding some from this decade.

A pounding on the door rang out into the silence, startling us both.

"Who's that?" Penelope asked, her fingers flying to clasp her bra as she sat up.

"I don't know, but I'll get rid of them," I told her, pulling my shirt over my head and shoving my feet into my boots.

"Should I stay here?"

"Yeah. It's safer out of sight until we know what we're dealing with."

She slipped on her sneakers and grabbed the fireplace poker. "Okay. I'm ready."

Amused, I eyed her fighting stance. "Ready for what? Who do you think is going to be out there?"

Penelope glared at me. "Just go answer the door, jerk. I want to know what a centuries-old demon does in a centuries-old bed."

I bowed, leering at her. "I am your servant to command, milady."

She smirked. "I want you to remember that you said that."

"I will," I promised, pressing my lips to hers before appearing before the door.

"I hate it when you do that!" she muttered from the bedroom.

Grinning, I unlocked the door and only had a split second of recognition before a blur of motion tackled me, pushing me a couple of steps back into the parlor.

"Rayonus!" the beautiful young demon cried. "You've come back!"

Of all the demons I thought might knock on my door, this female was one I hoped would have forgotten I existed. She had an uncanny way of showing up at my door when I came into town, and an even more mysterious way of getting me into her bed each time she did.

I cast a furtive look over my shoulder toward the bedroom. "Helisa, what are you doing here?"

The demon sighed and flicked long locks of white hair over her bare red-skinned shoulder. "My mother had a vision that you'd be in need of some of the spring water salt she brought back from her travels in Austria last year. I thought I'd make a house call and give it to you myself." She bared her fangs in a seductive smile and trailed a clawed finger down my abdomen to my waistband. "Along with anything else you want, of course."

Grabbing her wrist, I stopped her downward motion. "Helisa, I'm mated now."

She pouted prettily. "So am I, but that doesn't mean we can't have a little fun. Not that you've ever really been *little*."

"As much as that bolsters my ego, you know what you and Toraris have isn't a true mating. It's a convenient financial arrangement at best. My mate is for life."

She stepped back as if I'd slapped her. "You can't mean that, Rayonus. No demon mates for an immortal lifetime."

"I did, and so did my mate," Penelope said, coming out of the hallway in her demon form. With her long brown hair tousled and wild around her shoulders, her shirt still unbuttoned to show the sheer black bra she wore, and nothing but black lace panties covering her bottom half, she looked satisfied and well-laid.

Incredulous, Helisa asked, "Her, Rayonus? You're giving up our dalliances for a half-human?"

"Don't worry," a black-eyed, pissed off Penelope simpered. "I just *dallianced* his fucking brains out. He's all set."

Howling with rage, Helisa threw the burlap bag of salt at my chest and stormed out, yelling, "Find another salt supplier, Rayonus Rixa!"

In shock and in complete and total lust with Penelope, I closed and locked the door before turning on her. Her face was the picture of innocence.

"Dallianced my fucking brains out?" I asked, ripping my shirt off and stalking toward her.

Penelope shrugged as she quickly backed down the hallway. "You're my mate or whatever. The days of her enjoying your . . . uh, attributes are over. You're mine now."

"You want these attributes, little demon?" I growled, kicking off my jeans mere moments before I let my body change into its natural form.

"Why?" she sassed, slinging her bra and shirt to the floor and climbing onto the bed. "Are you going to give them to me?"

She let out a little yelp as I flipped her onto her back, then her lips parted in a very feminine gasp as I pressed myself between her legs. I shook my head and chuckled. "Oh, Penny, you have no idea how bad I'm going to give it to you."

CHAPTER 11

For two demons with jobs, responsibilities, and a task to do, Penelope and I were shameless in the way we whiled away the hours, learning each other's bodies as we frolicked in my oversized bed. It was somewhat of a novelty for her. For me, as well, but not in the same sense. The novelty for me was feeling that the woman in this ridiculously massive bed was made for me and me alone. No female I had ever known in the biblical sense had ever made me feel—had ever made me want—more from them. Penelope did. She was it for me. Woe be the idiot that ever tried to take her.

I let Penelope sleep for a few hours before I roused her into the shower and made us breakfast with items I popped out to get from my apartment. It wasn't out of the norm for me to be domestic at times, but waking up here at my home—my real home—with her in my arms had done something to me. It felt so surreal. After more than six hundred long years, I woke up with an overwhelming need to nourish my lover's body, to please her, to protect her in any way I could, even if that meant with my own life. These feelings scared me, and yet, they felt right.

"Morning," Penelope said, yawning as she toweled her hair dry.

Struck by how beautiful she was, I rounded the counter and fell to my knees. "Marry me, Penelope," I begged. "Be my wife and my mate."

"What, no ring?" she asked with amusement in her eyes.

Without a second thought, I took her hand and transported us to the master bedroom in my apartment in Havenwood Falls. Standing, I opened the top dresser drawer and grabbed the red velvet box containing my great-grandmother's ring.

When I faced Penelope, her eyes were wide with shock. She hadn't realized how serious I was about this, about us.

I opened the box and stared at the blood-red cinnabar crystal. "This ring has been passed down through my family for thousands of years. It hasn't always been a ring. It began as a pretty bauble in the hilt of a sword. It has been an amulet, talisman, a brooch, and even bargaining chip for someone's life in the years since. My grandmother passed it down to me. She didn't trust my mother not to sell or pawn it. Now I want you to have it. I want you to pass it down to our son or daughter when it is time and for them to pass it down to their sons and daughters." Meeting her eyes, I knelt again. "Be my wife. Dalliance my brains out on a regular basis."

She laughed and nodded with tears gathering in her eyes as she held out her hand. The metal sizzled as I settled it onto her finger, the magic protection spell conforming to her particular essence before glowing bright red and then dulling to its normal shade.

"Is that a yes?"

"Yes," she said, bending to give me a smacking kiss. "I will dalliance your brains out on a regular basis."

Standing, I gathered her into my arms and kissed her properly, our breath mingling, our tongues sweeping against each other's until she melted against me and I was panting with the effort to control the raging need to take her right here on the bedroom floor—again. "I love you, Penny."

"I love you, Rayonus," she replied, giving me another sweet kiss. "But didn't I smell pancakes at your other place?"

I laughed at the sudden change of topic. "My plans to ravish you are foiled by the siren call of pancakes. I should probably get used to this sort of thing, shouldn't I?"

She shrugged. "That probably wouldn't be such a bad idea."

~

Thirty minutes and four pancakes later, I coaxed Penelope away from the platter of bacon and into the street. With the sun shining and the merchants' wares laid out for everyone to see, it wasn't nearly as ominous as it looked when we arrived the night before. During the day, I didn't mind letting Penelope explore the stands and stores, oohing and aahing over every little thing she found interesting. She was adorable, really, my little demon mate.

Letting her visit every store she fancied, I kept a watch out for the items we needed and demons I knew that sold them. We had wound our way down to the river when I found just the demon I'd hoped we'd find easily. She had moved her shop from where it was the last time I'd stopped in, which was a very regular occurrence, but she couldn't hide the flashing green of her eyes under the red wool hood she wore. Even in her demon form, those eyes were unmistakable.

"Fyrira," I called, greeting her with a small bow. "It has been too long."

Her voice was hoarse and low when she answered but just as friendly and warm as it had been since I was a youngling. "That it has, Rayonus. That it has." She eyed Penelope, then gave me what I could only describe as a *you sly dog* look. "Who might this lovely half-demon accompanying you be?"

"This is my mate, Penelope. Penelope, this is Fyrira. She has sold Sicilian brimstone at the markets for as long as anyone can remember."

Penelope curtsied, making Fyrira and me chuckle with delight.

"Sorry," she said, laughing at herself. "I'm not sure what the procedure is when meeting new demons yet. Rayonus, as you can imagine, isn't the most thorough of teachers when it comes to manners."

"Truer words were never spoken about our little trickster, Rayonus," Fyrira croaked. "He does have quite the bad reputation."

I shook my head. "Hey. That hurts my feelings. I've always been good to both of you."

They both stared at me, stunned at what I'd just said.

"Okay, maybe not, but my heart's always in the right place."

They continued to stare.

Laughing, I held my hands up in defense. "Okay. Okay. I'm a recovering terrible demon."

"That's more like it," Penelope said, grinning at me like I was her whole world.

I liked that look. No. I loved it. I wanted her to never stop looking at me like that.

Fyrira watched us stare at each other for a long moment, then shook her head. "You two are more smitten than any demons I've ever seen."

"You haven't met Cameron and Mavis DeSalle," Penelope told her. "Those two are so sickeningly sweet, they'll give you a toothache."

"I find that hard to believe about the Exitium Daemonium and the son of Severin DeSalle," Fyrira replied sagely.

"Oh, no. It's true," I concurred. "They are disgustingly affectionate."

She barked out a rusty laugh and motioned us into her tent. "Come, younglings. If it's brimstone you need, it is brimstone you shall have."

After only a few minutes inside the tent, Penelope and I left to find the next piece to our puzzle, but not before Fyrira warned us that we had better watch ourselves while we were in the marketplace. "There are eyes and ears everywhere," she said. "Say anything interesting, do anything interesting, and they will hear and see you. Do not forget, younglings."

We agreed to stay on course after her dire warning, only visiting the tent Fyrira had directed us to for the African gum arabic made from an acacia tree. The salesman, Arlennear, a demon I'd known for decades, sold us the item without any conversation at all, handing it over immediately after accepting my offer of four gold coins with a nod.

The only thing left was for us to choose an amulet to hold the magic.

After looking in a few more stalls, Penelope pulled me to the side to whisper into my ear. "Do you think it's possible for me to use my ring as the amulet? It doesn't have to strictly be a necklace, does it?"

I grinned. "Of course it is. The cinnabar the ring is made from is a perfect conductor for demon magic."

With our last step decided, we hurried back to my home and collapsed on the stiff settee with our purchases laid out on the table before us.

"That was a bizarre day of shopping," Penelope said, rubbing her socked feet. "Demon shopping is not like human shopping."

"I agree wholeheartedly. There is a distinct lack of food courts in Patriam."

"Food sounds so good," she moaned, then she sat up suddenly. "Oh, my God! I forgot to tell Dao that I needed the night off!"

"What time is your shift?"

"Four to ten."

I checked my phone. "We can make it in time. But what about the seeing everyone in their true form thing?"

"Shit. I forgot about that. Nearly everyone here is already in their true form."

I nodded, agreeing with that assessment. Here they had nothing to hide, so most of the population didn't bother.

"So, what're you going to do?"

"What choice do I have?"

"This may be the terrible demon with the bad reputation in me, but you could call in sick and spend the night eating exotic demon delicacies with your fiancé. Technically, you are having a problem that keeps you from completing your work as usual. It's not that much of a stretch."

Penelope chewed her lip. "Can our phones work from here?"

"No, but the trip back to Havenwood Falls will only take a second," I said, standing up. "Ready?" I asked, pulling her to her feet.

She grabbed her shoes in one hand and threaded the fingers of her free hand with mine. "Ready."

We arrived in Penelope's apartment to a severely pissed off ice demon.

"Where the fuck have you been?" Mavis cried as soon as we popped into existence. "I've been worried out of my mind. Dao said you had to leave early the other night and asked me to check up on you yesterday. Yesterday! Where have you been?"

I rolled my eyes. "Calm down, Mom. I've been with her the whole time. She's perfectly fine."

"Funny, but that doesn't really do anything to calm me," she spat, yanking Penelope away from me.

"Are you okay?" she asked my mate. "He didn't put you in any danger, did he?"

"No. Actually, he's been helping me track down the items to help me make an amulet. The Alchemist refused to help and was all sketchy, so I'm just going to try to do it myself."

"You took her to Patriam to see her father?" Mavis asked me, her face incredulous. "Wait." She turned back to Penelope. "Why do you need an amulet, Penny?"

"Because I can see you. Like, the real demon you right now. Horns and all."

Mavis patted the top of her head and frowned. "How?"

Penelope shrugged and shook her head. "Apparently, it's my talent. That's why I had to leave work so abruptly. Dao's six tails were freaking me out. Not to mention, did you know there are werewolves in this town?"

"Just the sheriff and a shit ton of others," Mavis answered. "Can you see Ray's demon form right now?"

"Yeah, but I'm pretty used to that by now. It doesn't really freak me out. And that's a pretty good thing, since he's asked me to marry him."

Mavis's mouth dropped open with a squeak.

"Uh oh. I think we might have broken her," I said, waving a hand in front of her shocked face. "Quick, show her your demon form to snap her out of it."

If possible, Mavis's eyes widened even farther.

"You're scaring me," Penelope said, taking her arm to lead her to the couch. "Say something."

"Go get Cam," Mavis demanded of me. "Right now. I'm calling a family meeting."

CHAPTER 12

*O*nce we explained the situation and the shock of the engagement and seeing Penelope as a bronze-colored, fanged demon wore off, Mavis and Cam finally gathered enough sense between them to congratulate me and ask if Penny was out of her ever-loving mind.

"The ring is beautiful," Mavis whispered to Penelope. "And it's powerful to be sure; I can feel the magic pulsing in it. But are you sure Rayonus is the demon you want to spend an eternity with? We're talking about someone who has sold us out, betrayed us, and left us in the dark."

"Yes," she agreed. "But we're also talking about someone who risked his own life to end Severin's madness, worked hard to get back into our good graces, and loves me beyond reason."

"I just want to remind everyone that I'm sitting right here," I said sourly. "I also have feelings."

"Since when?" Cam asked.

I held up a middle finger to my best friend. "Right here, Cameron."

"Okay, that's enough of that," Penelope said, moving from the couch to the loveseat to sit with me. "Rayonus is a douchebag."

"Was a douchebag," I interrupted.

Mavis harrumphed. "Debatable."

Penelope rolled her eyes. "You guys know what I mean. He's changed, and not in the *I want to get in your pants* way. He's really an entirely different demon than we used to know."

"Regardless, he's not good enough for you," Cam said. "No offense, Rayonus."

I glared at him. "I'm taking full offense. You guys are supposed to be my friends."

"To be fair, it is Penny we're talking about," Cam said. "I'm not sure there's a creature, demon or human, that's good enough for her."

Penelope grinned at him. "Awww . . . I didn't know you cared."

"Yes, you did," Mavis countered. "He says it repeatedly."

"Okay, maybe I did, but it still makes me all squishy inside when he says it."

I sighed heavily, looking over my friends. I knew they meant well, and I knew they would come around, but it hurt me to know, when it came down to it, they didn't trust me. It was deserved—I knew that—but it still pained me in a way I never expected to feel.

"Getting back to the task at hand," I said. "Penny, unless you're okay with seeing a hell of a lot more creatures on your work shift, I suggest you go ahead and call in sick. Mom and Dad, are you coming to Patriam with us to see if we can make the amulet, or are you going to worry yourselves into an early grave?"

Cam shot a glowering look my way. "We're immortal, dickhead."

"I put nothing past you guys," I retorted.

"I've never been to Patriam," Mavis said, looking at her husband with excitement. "Can we go?"

"Is there a reason we have to do this in Patriam?" Cam asked.

"Well, not technically, but the ingredients are there, and the spell will most assuredly attract attention."

He sighed. "It's against all of my better judgment, but yes. We can go." When Mavis jumped up and down with excitement, he added, "As long as you don't wander off and get yourself in trouble.

Mavis scoffed. "I'm the Exitium Daemonium. Who's going to bother me?"

"Do you need a list?" I asked, thinking of the many, many demons who had protection amulets just like Severin DeSalle did before I took it.

"Exactly," Cameron said, pointing at me. "Let's not get too big for our britches."

Penelope laughed. "Cam, you're so old! Who says that anymore?"

"I'm old? Have you stopped to think about how old your fiancé is?" he retorted.

"I prefer experienced when it comes to Ray. Because wow, his—"

Cam held up his hands to stop her from speaking while Mavis plugged her ears with her fingers and started singing "Jingle Bells" as loud as she could.

I might have preened a bit.

Kissing my love's temple, I stood and pulled her to her feet. "If you guys are coming, let's do this. I have work tomorrow myself."

"Please?" Mavis pleaded. "You never take me anywhere."

"That's because we were kidnapped the last time I took you out of town. And you want to go to the demon underworld with the very guy who set that up?"

"I'm out of the kidnapping game," I told Cam. "You don't have to worry about that from me anymore."

He narrowed his eyes. "What do I have to worry about, then?"

"Premature balding? Impotence? How am I supposed to know?"

Penelope blanched. "And on that note, I say it's time to go." She held a hand out to Mavis. "Coming with us?"

Mavis batted her eyes. "Please, honey?"

"Fine," Cam growled. "But if we have to kill any demons, you're never going anywhere with Rayonus again."

She clapped her hands together and jumped up and down. "Yay! Underground trip!"

After Penelope made her phone call to Dao, I transported her to our home in Patriam, followed by Cam, and finally a giddy Mavis, all in the span of less than a minute. We weren't in a huge hurry, but the less time we all spent in the underground, the safer we would all be.

Cam was right to be leery. Mavis was a weapon that any demon would love to possess.

Once everyone was there, the tour of the home was complete, and the laughter died down about the massive bed in the bedroom, we got down to brass tacks.

"Do I need to take the ring off for this to work or do we do it while it's on?" Penelope wondered aloud, nervously twisting my grandmother's ring around her finger.

I checked the pictures on the phone, translating the Latin as fast as I could. "I think we need to put it on a natural, non-synthetic surface."

"What about the slate fireplace?" Cam suggested.

I nodded, reading a bit more. "That should work."

"What's next?" Mavis asked, her eyes alight with excitement. "Sacrifice a goat? Dance around naked under the stars?"

We all stared at her.

"What? Isn't that what demons do?"

"In the movies, maybe," I said, laughing at her crestfallen expression. "This is a little more straightforward. We're not depending on anything else to give us the power. It's all inside Penelope."

Mavis looked expectantly at me.

I frowned. "What?"

"No sexual innuendo? You literally just said, 'It's all inside Penelope.' I'm finding it a little hard to believe that you were able to control yourself with that kind of opening."

"You said opening," Penelope told her, giggling so hard she fell into me.

Mavis slapped a hand across her eyes. "Never mind. I see Penny has picked up the passed torch with the innuendos."

"Hey! Someone has to do it!" she exclaimed. "We cannot live in an innuendo-less world. Right, babe?"

Cam gave me a look of disgust. "You did this."

I kissed Penelope's smiling mouth and shook my head. "No, Cam. Some things are just meant to be."

He rolled his eyes. "Can we move this along before Mavis decides to venture outside of your, frankly, quaint home? The giant-sized bed will only keep her entertained for a few minutes."

Mavis rolled her eyes, then shrugged. "He's probably right. So, we've got the ring in a pure, non-synthetic place. What's the next step?"

I handed the bag of salt to Penelope. "Sprinkle the salt over the cinnabar and the silver ring. When it's completely covered, say *purgo* to purify it."

She nodded and started pouring the salt. "Mavis, remind me to tell you about Ray's demon ex-girlfriend that literally threw this salt at him. That exchange was one for the books."

I laughed. "That it was. Helisa is probably still fuming over it."

"A good demon dick is hard to find," she said in a commiserating voice. "I almost feel sorry for taking hers."

"Second that," Mavis piped up. "But, you know, not the taking your dick part, Ray."

Cameron groaned. "This will never get done with the two of them together."

"It's a distinct possibility," I agreed, handing Penelope the gum arabic once she had spoken the first word of magic. "Make a well in the middle of the salt and add this. Once you're done, say *sorbere*. That will make the spell stick."

Her eyes widened as she spoke the second word. "I can feel it, Ray. It's pulling the magic from me."

"That means you have the same abilities as your father. Let us thank the stars he didn't raise you here himself. If he had, you would be enslaved. I have no doubt about that."

"What's the next word?" Mavis asked, leaning away from the red-glowing salt pile.

"*Simil.* It means to combine. You should be able to really feel the magic pull when you say this part, so immediately after, I want you to say *duco.* That will draw the extra power needed from the brimstone. Otherwise, there's a strong possibility that it could drain you for an extended amount of time."

Penelope spoke the words fast and deliberate, one of her hands holding tightly to me. As soon as she was done, a whoosh of heated air swept across the room, covering us with fine particles of the salt.

"What now, Ray?" Penelope asked, the light of the magic making her eyes glow in the semi-darkness of the parlor.

"*Minuas*," I told her. "That will diminish the magic that allows you to see a creature's true form. *Protego* will add protection."

"*Minuas!*" she exclaimed, her voice reverberating inside my head. "*Protego!*"

An explosion of light blinded us as the magic coursed from Penelope to the ring, and I felt her tighten her grasp against my forearm.

"Ray! I can't see!" she screamed.

I felt for her face and rained kisses over her tear-stained cheeks. "This will pass, my love. The same thing happened when Draz made my amulet."

She tucked her face into the crook of my neck. "I'm scared."

"I'm right here," I said, feeling around for Mavis and Cam without being able to see them. "Is that you, Mavis?"

"Why did I think this was a good idea?" Mavis groaned, wrapping her arms around us to join our person pretzel.

Cam sighed and threw his arms around the lot of us. "No one ever listens to me."

Penelope started to laugh. Then continued to laugh until our eyes adjusted and the tears on her cheeks were no longer tears of fear but mirth. She lifted her head and looked at us before picking up the ring. "Here goes nothing, I guess."

We collectively held our breath as the ring sizzled and popped down the length of her long finger.

"Well?" I asked expectantly.

She squinted at each of us, then grinned and threw her arms around me. "It worked!"

We all breathed a sigh of relief.

"Awesome," Cam said. "Not that this hasn't been fun and your house isn't lovely, Rayonus, but can we get the fuck out of here? Having Mavis in the underground is making me nervous."

I smiled at my old friend and clapped him on the back. "Sure, but I might remind you that you married this firecracker. You'll be dealing with her wants and wishes for the next few millennia, no matter how crazy they are."

Mavis slid her arms around her husband. "I knew I should've added that to my vows."

He cupped her face. "You missed your chance, you little hellion."

She smiled and stood on her tiptoes to give him a peck on the lips. "Drat."

"I can take you back when you're ready, Mavis."

"Wait a minute," she said, running toward the bedroom. We all heard the telltale click of her phone's camera before she ran back into the room, grinning from ear to ear. "Okay. I'm good."

"Don't get any ideas," Cam told her. "Neither one of us is a seven-foot-tall demon."

She shrugged and winked at him. "Not since you got your soul back, no, but I can think of a few ways to use that giant bed to our advantage . . . a few dirty, sexy ways."

I shivered. "Let's take that grossness back to your apartment, you two."

"Bye, guys!" Penelope called. "See you tonight for Napoli's and *Supernatural*?"

"Sounds good," Mavis said. "If you can tear yourself away from Mr. Wonderful for two seconds."

I beamed at Penelope. I'd never seen such a beautiful face on anyone before. "I have an eternity to spend with Penny watching *Supernatural* reruns," I told Mavis. "She can do whatever she likes as long as she comes home to me."

Cam held up a finger. "Speaking of that. You two have an extra apartment now. What are you going to do?"

Everything had happened in such a blur, I hadn't even considered the implications of our engagement, much less what our life would be like after the wedding. My place was nice here and I would never give it up, but Penny belonged in Havenwood Falls. She grew up there. It was home for both of us now.

"Penelope is the boss," I told him. "All decisions filter through my bride-to-be."

"Wow," Mavis marveled. "You have it really bad, Ray."

I smiled at Penny. "It doesn't look so bad from where I'm standing."

"Me either," she said, pulling me down to whisper in my ear. "I'll meet you in the bedroom when you get back."

Pulling her to me, I kissed her hard. "Give me thirty seconds and be naked."

"Ewwwww," Cam and Mavis chorused.

CHAPTER 13

I transported Mavis back to her house in Havenwood Heights, followed by Cam. They surprised me by giving me a hug before I could go back to Penelope.

"I'm really happy for both of you," Cameron said. "I know we've had our differences over the last year, but deep, deep, DEEP down, you've always been a stand-up guy."

"Don't lie to the demon," Mavis said, rolling her eyes. She put her hands on her hips and stared me down. "If you hurt her, I will make sure you suffer before I murder you right where you stand. Got it?"

I smirked. "Yes, Mother."

She smacked my chest. "Don't sass your mother."

I laughed. "Yes, ma'am."

"Now go back to Patriam before she thinks you've forgotten she's naked and waiting on you."

"Ugh," Cam groaned. "I wish *I* could forget about that."

With a wave, I stepped back from the pair and traveled back to my house in the underground.

"Penny? I'm back," I called, knowing before I even got the words out that something was wrong.

"Penelope?"

When there was no answer, I appeared in the bedroom. She wasn't there. Popping into the bathroom to find it empty broke something inside of me. Where was she? Had she left of her own volition, or had she been taken?

"Penelope!" I screamed, hearing my voice crack. I'd never been so scared, so panicked. I had to find her.

Racing to the front door, I found something I hoped I wouldn't find. Antimony, also known as kohl to humans, was semi-poisonous to demons of every kind. Most were wary of even touching it, for fear they would succumb to its sedative properties accidentally. But there was one demon that used common poisons all the time. I would delight in watching the light leave his eyes if he was behind this.

The Alchemist.

"Fuck!" I yelled, punching the wall as I shifted into my true form. If he hurt her—if he did anything to her—I would make what Sam and Dean did to demons on *Supernatural* look tame.

Snatching the door open, I slammed it behind me and stormed down the packed street. No one tried to stop me. Some even pointed me in the direction of Draz's home to stay on my good side, assuming I had one. The demons who had witnessed my raw power centuries ago knew better than to hide her from me. Demons were devious and selfish, not stupid. They knew that immortality could be snuffed out in less than a second.

A block away from the alleyway, I bellowed, "Draz! Show yourself to me or suffer my fucking wrath! I will only ask once!"

The demons interested enough to have followed my path at a distance scurried away from me when they caught sight of the raging lunatic I was rapidly becoming. Even with the amulet on, my magic surged, twisting and turning, coiling like a snake within me. It stole my reason, my sanity. All my magic knew was that he had kidnapped its mate. The mate we'd fought for. The mate we'd killed for. The mate that completed us unlike any other female ever had. Our vengeance would be an ugly, horrible thing to behold, and it would hurt.

"DRAZ!" I screamed outside his door, pounding on it so hard the hinges were buckling under my fists.

When he didn't answer, I snapped. Ripping the dampening amulet off my neck, I threw it to the ground and crushed it beneath my heel. The time for asking was over. I would destroy everything he held dear, everything he'd worked for. He would know destruction, and its name would be Rayonus.

For the first time in centuries, the real power that resided in me flared to life and vibrated wild and untamed. The hunger of the destructive beast released. It wanted to taste the blood of my enemies, rip their bodies to shreds, and bring the world to collapse around their broken and battered corpses.

Focused like I'd never been before, I roared as I shot my magic into the door. It disintegrated.

Smiling with malevolence, I ducked to step into the space where the door had been and caught Draz's arm as he came at me with a blade. His bloodcurdling scream was the thing of nightmares as I crushed his arm into fragments with nothing more than a thought. Shoving him to the ground, I kicked the blade aside and loomed over him, fangs bared.

"Where is she?" I demanded, grabbing his hair to keep him from scrambling away from me. "WHERE?"

"I'm here, baby," Penelope's tired voice answered. "But I'm not sure where here is and why this black powdery stuff on my face is making me so sleepy."

"Penelope," I breathed out, taking in every single, minute thing about her. My eyes couldn't get enough of her.

She frowned. "Where's your amulet?"

"I destroyed it, just like I will destroy all the demons that try to keep you from me." I turned to look at a cowering Draz on the floor before bringing my attention back to her. "Starting with him."

Her brows shot up. "Is there any way we can *not* do that?"

My growl shook the bricks around us. "He drugged you with antimony! He took you away from our home! On my honor, I will crush his bones to dust!"

Penelope held her hands in the universal position for a time out. "Rayonus, you don't need to do that. There are worse ways to hurt him," she said, glaring at him with fury as hot as lava in her eyes. "Much more long-lasting and permanent ways."

Draz whimpered as he clutched his shattered arm to his chest. "Please, child. I'm sorry for what I've done. Believe me, daughter."

"He lies!" I thundered, lifting him up by his throat and slamming him against the wall. He collapsed bonelessly in a heap at my feet. I reached for him again.

"Rayonus! No!" Penelope shrieked, throwing inky powder in my face.

I only had time to realize that she'd used the antimony on me before my legs crumpled and I crashed to the floor.

I woke to the sound of angels. Well, if angels sang like a cross between a rabid cat and Alanis Morissette on her worst day.

"Oh, good," Penelope said, turning down her iPod. "You're finally awake."

Groggy and disoriented, I sat up and looked around. We were in Penelope's bedroom. "What happened?"

She climbed onto the bed, kissing me on the cheek before she settled cross-legged at the end of her bed. "What do you remember?"

I furrowed my brow, thinking back to what I'd done—everything that had happened once I found out she was missing. "I remember . . . everything. How is that possible?"

"I'd tell you if I knew," she said, shrugging. "Your amulet is right there."

I followed her line of sight to the crushed amulet laying on the bedside table. "But . . . I'm lucid. I'm focused."

She held her hands up. "I don't know how. I don't know why. But I'm not about to look a gift horse in the mouth."

"What about Draz? I didn't . . ."

"No. He's currently super pissed and wondering how his little girl knew how to bind his power without him sharing any family secrets."

My mouth dropped open. "You sly thing. You didn't."

Penelope scoffed. "The fuck I didn't. I ran and got Fyrira from the river, and she found a suitable crystal while I gathered the ingredients that we left at your house. It was said and done in less than five minutes."

Suitably impressed, I grinned at her, though my head felt like someone had screwed it on wrong. "Is he still bound?"

Shaking her head, she leaned onto her knees to reach a rolled up parchment next to the broken amulet. "I traded it back for this."

Unrolling the document, I squinted my blurry eyes and tried to make out the calligraphy.

"I can't see it quite yet," I told her, handing it over.

"It basically says that Draz is selling me to one Rayonus Rixa in exchange for his magic to be unbound—in blood, which is fucking gross."

I shook my head, not understanding. "What do you mean, he sold you to me?"

"He was powerless. I made him an offer he couldn't refuse. My freedom for his. All he had to do was sever the ties to my blood with his blood on the contract, and it was a done deal. I was pretty offended by the whole selling part at first, but Fyrira assured me it's a pretty common practice between parents and younglings within the demon community. She's a smart lady."

"Smarter than I realized," I said absently.

"She also advised me to keep our little arrangement just between us and not tell Mavis and Cam. Well, she called him the incubus. At first, I thought maybe it was because Mavis might be pissed enough to go to Patriam and strike down demons like it was some biblical reckoning, but I think she just knew they'd be over here telling us 'I told you so' until we both went into convulsions. Either way, the demon is a literal lifesaver."

I chuckled, sitting up straighter as I started to regain my strength. "It seems we owe Fyrira a debt of gratitude."

Penelope curled into my side, wrapping my arm around her like a security blanket. "Definitely. And she also kind of insisted we name our first daughter after her, but honestly, I can't think of a better name than that of the demon who saved us from certain doom and had a hand in me gaining my freedom from a real douchebag." She leaned away from me to look me in the eyes. "If you know any other jackass demons like him, I don't care what we think we might need. I don't want to meet them—ever."

Pulling her close, I brushed back the mane of tangled hair in her face and kissed her as tenderly as I could manage with the emotions growing inside of me. "That is a promise I would love to keep. As is naming our child after Fyrira. But I hope you know that I never want you indebted to me. If we didn't need this paper, I would burn it to ash right now."

Penelope shrugged and nipped at my lips before straddling me and laying a kiss on me so hot it sent shockwaves through my body. "That's too bad, you know, because as my mate, you're always going to own a piece of my heart."

Sliding my hands down to cup her ass, I said, "If that's the case, we're indebted to each other."

"Good," she purred. "Because I want to dalliance your brains out for the rest of my life."

I grinned, flipping her onto her back. "Not if I dalliance your brains out first."

We hope you enjoyed this story in the Havenwood Falls series featuring a variety of supernatural creatures. The series is a collaborative effort by multiple authors. You might also enjoy JD Nelson's other stories in the Havenwood Falls universe:
Plans Laid Bare
Soul Laid Bare

You may also enjoy these books in the main Havenwood Falls series:

Ink & Fire by R.K. Ryals
Tragic Ink by Heather Hildenbrand

Nowhere to Hide by Belinda Boring
The Lurkers Within by Danielle Bannister
Of Salt and Stars by Seven Jane

Also try the YA line, Havenwood Falls High; the historical paranormal line, Legends of Havenwood Falls; and the darker, sexier side of town, Havenwood Falls Sin & Silk.

Stay up to date at www.HavenwoodFalls.com

ABOUT THE AUTHOR

JD Nelson is a Bestselling Author of Fantasy Romance and Adult Paranormal Romance. An avid time-waster, JD enjoys watching TV and listening to audiobooks when she really should be writing.

JD loves to hear from her readers. You can contact her through her website, AuthorJDNelson.com, or on Facebook, where she spends an alarming amount of time chatting with her many author and reader friends, much to the dismay of her continually neglected manuscripts.

ACKNOWLEDGMENTS

To the readers, thank you for asking for more of Ray and Penelope's story! I couldn't have written this without your support and feedback!

AN EXCERPT

Plans Laid Bare (A Havenwood Falls Sin & Silk Novella) by J.D. Nelson

Mavis LeGrand had always suspected her grandfather was a little off, and when he suddenly moved them to a remote town in Utah, her suspicions rose. Nevertheless, she lived a typical life—high school, friends, and eventually college in the small but safe town he'd chosen. But when she finds his journal after a life-altering accident, she learns the hard truth—her grandfather isn't human, and neither is she.

She also discovers his plans to use her power in the evil scheme he's been arranging since her infancy.

Knowing her very existence depends on him never finding her, Mavis makes her escape and hitches a ride with the devilishly handsome half incubus, Cameron DeSalle. Despite her initial trepidation, she instantly feels a connection with him and believes him when he says he'll do everything in his power to protect her.

Mavis finds herself falling for Cameron, the ice in her veins melting away with every heated look and stolen kiss. But whether Cameron feels the same desire for her or it's his incubus nature bringing them closer, Mavis isn't sure. The only thing she knows for certain is until they defeat her grandfather, they'll never have a happily ever after.

PLANS LAID BARE

"Shit! Shit! Shit!" I muttered, frantically shoving the clothes from the laundry basket into my backpack. I had to do this faster. "Think! Think, Mavis! You can do this!"

I blew out a breath, trying to calm myself enough to concentrate on what I needed to do next. Everything was moving so fast. I couldn't grab hold of the thoughts racing through my head. How could this be happening to me?

Stopping, I closed my eyes and took a deep, cleansing breath. I needed clarity, focus. And I needed it yesterday.

I opened my eyes. Money. I was going to need lots of money.

Straightening the room as I went, I stopped at the door to look for anything out of place. The room was messy, as usual, but not I-packed-my-whole-world-in-three-minutes messy. He was used to seeing this level of clutter.

This will work, I thought. *It has to work.*

Throwing my backpack over my shoulder, I set out at a brisk pace, making a beeline to the jar of mad money he kept on top of the refrigerator. As tempted as I was to take it all, I didn't. I had to make sure nothing was amiss. If anything was different, if anything caught his eye, he would know, and he would come for me. That couldn't happen. Having a decent head start would mean the difference between life and death.

~

I ran until I couldn't run anymore. My feet ached. My mouth was as dry as the Sahara Desert. My clothes were dirty and torn from ducking behind trees and diving into ditches in blind, terrified panic. And I was tired. We're talking the weary-to-the-bone kind of tired. The kind of exhaustion you feel when you've been down with the flu for three days and try to do something normal . . . like breathe.

I smiled bitterly as I kicked a rock, listening to it skitter down the pavement into the darkness beyond. I knew I would never have to worry about something as mundane as the flu again. Because, as of two hours earlier, I had learned the truth about myself. I'd never been normal. I was as far away from ordinary as I could be. I was an ice demon.

Yes, an ice demon. Me, Mavis LeGrand, college graduate, ex-cheerleader, and high school debate club president, a demonic entity.

Of all the absurd things I thought could happen to me, finding out I was a creature of Hell hadn't even been on the list. The mere idea was ludicrous. Before this afternoon, my life had been boring. There'd been no excitement, no surprises. And no one could have had a more idyllic upbringing than I had. Sure, the thing pretending to be my grandfather had been a little cold and creepy, but a demon with a propensity for evil? Not in a million years would I have suspected him of that.

I snorted to myself, almost delirious in my exhaustion. As if any of that stuff still mattered. That fake life was over. It didn't exist anymore. And it never would again.

The faint glow of headlights in the distance pulled me out of my misery and set my heart racing. Darting to my right, I dove headfirst into a deep and, thankfully, grassy ditch and prayed that the vehicle wouldn't stop. I'd come so far. I couldn't let my grandfather find me after everything I'd been through tonight.

I tried to hold my breath as the sound of the tires grew closer, but a sharp sob tore out of me on its own volition when I heard the telltale squeak of the brakes and a door opening. All the effort, all the ridiculous abuse I'd put my body through—it was for nothing. He'd found me. My grandfather had found me.

"I'm not one to pry into someone else's business," an unfamiliar voice drawled, "but I've got to tell you, when I saw you take that Olympic dive into the drainage ditch, I had questions. Mainly, what the hell is that little blond woman doing?"

With tears streaming down my face, I sat up to see a pair of black boots come to a stop in the gravel in front of me. Though I couldn't make out his features with his truck's headlights shining so brightly behind him, I knew he was smiling down at me. I could hear humor in his deep, gruff voice.

"Aw, coach, I'm just practicing for the next meet," I told him, damn close to hyperventilating. "We're going to bring home the gold this year!"

The man's sharp bark of a laugh made me jump.

"You do that now," he said.

I grinned. "I'll give it my best shot."

"I never had a doubt. But before you do that, why don't I give you a ride somewhere. Where're you headed?"

"It doesn't matter," I said truthfully. "Anywhere that's out of town."

"Well, then, you're in luck. I happen to be heading in that direction."

I pursed my lips, weighing my options. Hitchhiking with a stranger was crazy. I knew it. He knew it. Everyone knew it. But the urge to take him up on his offer was overwhelming. The man did seem genuinely concerned by my ditch antics.

But still, my grandfather didn't raise a fool.

"How do I know I can trust you?" I asked him, narrowing my eyes.

"You don't. But riding with me is better than risking a rattlesnake bite every time a truck comes down the road, right? And I promise to behave myself, so what do you have to lose?"

I had to admit, even in early October, he had a point about those snakes. I didn't know how many more times I could repeat my swan-dive-into-questionable-ditches routine without suffering serious injury.

"Okay," I said finally. "Thanks."

Crouching down, he reached out a hand to help me up. "Here, let me give you a . . . shit." He stood up quickly. "Get down. Someone's coming."

Lying flat, I watched the man step closer to the edge and move his hands to his fly.

"What are you doing?" I hissed.

"Saving your ass," he whispered. "Now lie still. They won't stop if they think I'm taking a piss."

Closing my eyes, I concentrated on the crunch of crisp leaves as the vehicle slowly approached.

"Evening," I heard my would-be savior call. "Do you want to hold it for me or something?"

I trembled uncontrollably as a scolding, laced with obscenities, erupted from the driver. It was him. My grandfather had found me.

"Don't let him see me," I whispered as the car sped off. "Please."

"Come on, then," he said, squatting down to reach for me. "Hurry up."

I took the hand he offered and shouted, "Oh!" when a warm jolt of electricity traveled up the length of my arm.

"Sorry," he said apologetically. "I wasn't expecting you to be an immortal," he explained. "Humans can't feel that. I was trying to put you at ease."

"Put me at ease? What just happened?"

"I'm a cambion," he said simply, as if that would explain everything.

"A what?"

"I'll tell you in the truck." He opened the passenger side door. "We need to get going, in case he doubles back."

I nodded and quickly brushed the debris from my clothes, not knowing what to think about his revelation. Was a cambion a demon like myself or something different? Was he dangerous? Did that even matter? Whether he killed me or my impostor grandfather did, I was still one dead demon chick.

Finally, I decided to throw caution to the wind and climbed into the truck. Buckling my seatbelt, I waited for him to get in on the driver's side before I blurted out, "I'm an ice demon."

"Those are rare," he replied, nonplussed.

"Are they? Do you know anything about them?"

He chuckled and cranked his truck. "Don't you?"

I shook my head. "No. I just found out I was a demon, oh . . ." I checked my nonexistent watch. "About two hours ago. I'm hoping the learning curve isn't steep."

"What's your name?" he asked, whipping the truck around to head for the interstate.

"Mavis LeGrand."

He nodded, leaning over to switch on the interior light. "I'm Cam, Cameron DeSalle. Pleased to meet you."

I blinked a few times, letting my eyes adjust to the sudden brightness. Then I lost my power of speech. My Good Samaritan was a dark angel in tight blue jeans.

A furrow appeared between his brows. "Are you okay, Mavis?"

"Y-yeah, I just didn't expect . . ." I threw my hands up. "Cameron, you're like, crazy hot. You know that, right?"

He laughed. "Yes, but I don't think anyone has ever told me quite so bluntly."

"I'm sorry." I groaned, covering my face and lamenting my idiocy for a moment until I remembered how filthy my hands were and jerked them away from my face so fast, I accidentally hit one against the dash. When I looked up, nursing my aching hand to my chest, Cameron was staring at me with surprised amusement.

"You are a very entertaining ice demon," he told me.

"Thank you. And I'm sorry." I laughed. "It has been a day, and after everything else, I wasn't expecting someone so . . ."

"Attractive?" he asked. "Sexy? Irresistible?"

I gestured at his square jaw, thick black hair, and kind honey-brown eyes that would make any woman's panties melt right off. "Well, yeah. I mean, look at you, Cameron."

"Call me Cam," he reminded me.

"Okay. Cam the cambion, you're a regulation hottie. What's up with that?"

He groaned. "Come on, Mavis. A *Mean Girls* reference? I thought you were better than that."

"Then you thought wrong, because I'm really not," I told him, feeling almost hopeful for the first time since my world fell apart. "Now spill. What's it like to walk around with a mug like that twenty-four seven?"

"What's it like to walk around looking as pretty as you do?" he shot back.

"First off, don't even; I'm not the same caliber as you," I said. "And second, quit deflecting. I want an answer. Do women follow you around like the Pied Piper or what?"

He blew out a very put-upon sigh and leaned back in his seat. "Women are often attracted to me, yes."

"Knew it," I said smugly.

"It's not as if I want them to," he said, suddenly sitting upright. "I don't have a choice. My father is an incubus."

I blanched. "An incubus? Like, the steal-souls-by-having-sex kind of incubus I've read about in books?"

He gave me a winsome smile. "Yes. And that is a very accurate description."

"Do you do that? Steal souls, I mean."

He answered without the slightest bit of guilt. "Yes, but don't worry. You have nothing to fear from me."

"And why is that?" I asked, more than a little wary after his frank admission.

Cameron's dark eyes scanned my face for a moment before he turned his attention back to the road. "Because you don't have a soul, Mavis."

"I don't have a soul?" I asked in disbelief.

He shook his head. "Not that I can detect, no."

I sat back against the seat in stunned silence, wondering how this could be my life. Everything had been so boringly normal the day before. It was like I woke up in the twilight zone.

"I'm sorry," he said sheepishly. "That must have been a shock for you. I wasn't thinking."

"It's okay," I told him, my eyes welling up with tears again. "There's nothing to be done about it. It is what it is."

"There's a bottle of water in the glove compartment," he offered, looking at me as if he didn't know what to do about the dirty, tear-stained mess next to him.

Numb, I nodded and woodenly reached for the latch. I didn't know what to do about me, either.

"You're going to be okay," he said gently. "You're still the same demon you were yesterday. You just didn't know it yet."

I closed my eyes and inhaled deeply through my nose, holding it in a few seconds before exhaling. "Thank you, Cameron."

His expression turned serious as he clicked off the light. "It's no problem, but you do realize you're going to have to tell me what's going on, don't you? Obviously, you're in some trouble."

I pressed my lips together. As important as this was, it was hard to say something when you didn't want to hear it out loud. Hearing it out loud made it real. I wasn't ready for real yet.

"Come on," he urged. "I'm invested in this thing now. I want to help you. And that means I have to know who you're running from, so I can keep both of us safe."

"Okay," I said, straightening in my seat to face him. "I'll tell you, but only because I need help. And Cameron, if you're offering it to me, I'm going to take it. I don't have a choice. I don't think I can do this on my own." I blew out a shaky breath. "So, are you sure you want to help me?"

"I am," he said without hesitation. Then he pulled to the side of the road and shifted the truck into park. "Tell me how to help you, Mavis."

Wrapping my arms around myself, I sank back into my seat,

staring at the road stretching out in front of us. "I'm running from my grandfather."

"Your grandfather?" Cameron asked incredulously. "Why on Earth would you do that?"

I met his gaze. "Because he's not my grandparent. He's not even related to me. He's an ice demon, and he's planning on killing me."

≈

I thought Cam would insist I get out of his truck—that he'd leave me in his dust. But he didn't. Instead, he asked, "Did you just say your pretend grandfather is planning to kill you?"

I nodded, trying hard to keep eye contact. "Apparently, I'm the Exitium Daemonium."

His eyes widened. "The Exitium Daemonium? Like *the* Exitium Daemonium? Are you serious?"

"One hundred percent serious," I told him glumly.

"So the prophecy is true," he said, more to himself than me.

"I guess. I know less than nothing about the whole thing. What do you know about it?" I asked.

"Same as any demon knows. The Exitium Daemonium will bring death and destruction to demonkind."

I rolled my eyes. "Look at me, Cam. Do I look like I'm going to bring death and destruction to demonkind?"

"No, you look like an extremely filthy librarian."

"I rest my case."

"How did you find out?"

"I had an accident today."

"Like a car accident or an I-killed-a-demon type of accident?"

As his words sank in, my heart began to thump wildly. "Do you really think I can kill a demon?"

He laid a hand on top of mine to stop my fidgeting with the cap on the water bottle. "Mavis, if what you're saying is true, you're the ultimate in demon destruction."

"That's the thing," I said, ignoring the zing of energy that shot through me when he touched my skin. "I don't feel like hurting any demons. I feel stronger and keep having cold flashes since the accident, but I'm not having homicidal urges or anything."

"I think you'd better start at the beginning."

"Okay." I took a deep breath. "Late this afternoon, I fell down a huge flight of stairs at the public library, and when I was rushed to the hospital and x-rayed for suspected broken ribs, they found this weird anomaly that looked like it was encasing my heart, so they did an MRI."

"What did they find?"

"Nothing from the MRI. The machine blew up the second they turned it on. The explosion should have killed me, or at the least, burned me, but nothing happened. During all the confusion, smoke, and sirens, I ran."

"And since then you've felt stronger and have been feeling cold?"

I nodded. "I ran all the way from just south of Provo and never broke a sweat."

His mouth dropped open. "But that's forty miles from here. You've been jumping into ditches for forty miles?"

"Or ducking behind trees, or mailboxes, or cars. Whatever kept me from being seen."

He shook his head in wonder. "So, this anomaly, it had to be a throttle of some sort, right?"

"A throttle? Do you think that's what it was?"

"I do. There's no other way you wouldn't have noticed by now your ability to manipulate the cold. Did you get a chance to see the anomaly on the x-rays?"

"Unfortunately, yes. I'm pretty sure it's going to haunt my dreams."

"What did it look like?"

"Something diamond-shaped with runes engraved into it," I answered. "I couldn't tell what it was made of, though."

"Do you know anything about the runes that were on there?"

"See, that's where this whole thing got even more freaky. When I was little, I stumbled across a set of journals that had the same runes on them in my grandfather's study. He was pissed when he saw me playing with them, so the memory sort of sticks out to me. As soon as I saw the x-ray, I knew there had to be a connection, and I knew I needed to find those journals."

Cam looked suitably impressed. "And did you find them?"

I stared down at his big hand still covering my small ones. It was warm, comforting, and sending a flow of energy through me so filled with slow-burning desire, I almost hoped he'd never move it.

"Mavis?" he prompted.

"I did sneak into his library to read them," I said, finally meeting his eyes. "But I wasn't able to get past the first one before I knew I had to get out of the house. I had to get as far away from him as possible. Whoever he is, he isn't my real grandfather. He stole me from the underworld when I was an infant. He has plans to . . . He plans to . . ." I broke off, not able to finish the sentence. The horror of what I'd read was too fresh to talk about just yet.

He squeezed my hand briefly, then turned his attention back to the road. "There's a cheap motel up ahead," he said, throwing the truck into gear. "We can figure out what to do next once we're there."

I sighed in relief. "Thanks, Cam."

"Trust me. I'm doing this for me as much as I'm doing it for you. We can't let you fall into the wrong hands."

I frowned. "You say that like I'm some sort of weapon."

He caught my gaze as we passed under a streetlamp. "Not some weapon, Mavis, *the* weapon. I have to protect you in any way I can. There's no choice here. My own immortal life could depend on your safety."

I swallowed hard and nodded my acquiescence. Cam was right. I just hoped like hell my new friend would be up for the task.

Cameron parked his truck behind the Starlight Motel after making a pit stop at an all-night burger place. He left me eating a large order of fries and slamming a thirty-two-ounce soda while he checked us in.

Five minutes later, we were inside room seventeen, staring awkwardly at each other.

The room was clean and tastefully decorated with the latest in hotel chic. And me? I was incredibly dirty and feeling filthier by the second.

"I'm going to shower," I told him, grabbing my backpack. "I'll be right back."

"Take your time," he said through a mouthful of bacon cheeseburger. "Do you need clothes? They might be a little big, but I think I have a pair of sweats and a T-shirt that will do."

I had a few moments of pure yearning as I looked over to the overnight bag he was pointing to. What would it be like to be warm and wrapped up safe with his manly scent all over my body?

"Mavis?"

My cheeks heated up with a blush, and I sputtered, "Thank you. But I packed extra clothes in my backpack. I'm all right."

He nodded and helped himself to a handful of my uneaten fries. "Have a nice swim, then."

Once inside the bathroom with the door locked behind me, I twisted on the shower taps and braced my arms on the vanity.

"You will not think about how hot he is," I told the wistful, gray-eyed girl in the mirror. "You will ignore the unbelievable hotness."

And I did. For the next half hour, I didn't think about anything but the methodical process of washing the dirt from my body. When I was squeaky clean and feeling a hundred pounds lighter, I toweled off, brushed my teeth and hair, and dressed in clean yoga pants and a V-neck sleepshirt. I stepped out of the steamy bathroom looking and feeling like a new demoness.

Cameron had made himself at home while I showered. Lounging on the bed in gray sweatpants and a Smashing Pumpkins T-shirt, he was just putting down his cell phone and picking up the remote to flip through the channels on the ancient TV when I walked into the bedroom.

"Feel better?" he asked, barely glancing up.

I sat cross-legged on the opposite bed, facing him. "A whole lot better. Thank you."

He muted the TV and faced me, propping his head up on an elbow. "Well, well, well . . . you clean up nicely."

"Thanks," I said, looking away from his raised shirt and the tanned, lightly haired expanse of his stomach that was on full and glorious display.

"Very nicely," he mused. "I think you might be wrong about us not being the same caliber."

I didn't look away from the tacky hotel bedspread, but I could feel the weight of his scrutiny on me. And it did . . . things to me—bad things, naughty things.

He chuckled darkly, knowing precisely what I was thinking. "So, tell me about yourself, Mavis LeGrand, ice demon and Exitium Daemonium."

Shrugging, I met his lazy gaze. "There's not that much to tell. I got my MBA from the University of Utah and have—*had*—a good paying job. I was living a totally normal human life. Three hours later, here we are."

"That would make you, what, twenty-two or twenty-three, right?"

"I'm twenty-six. How old are you?"

"Older than twenty-six," he evaded.

I shook my head, smiling at him. "That means you're really old and don't want to tell me, doesn't it?"

He returned my smile. "Something like that."

"Do you plan on being this evasive all night?"

"Not at all," he said. "I plan to sleep at some point."

"Funny."

He clicked off the TV, leaving us in the dim light of the lamp between our beds. "So, what does a twenty-six-year-old college graduate do for money these days?"

"Well, this one was given an accounting job with her grandfather's firm in New York. I telecommute Monday through Friday. The job is a waste of my degree, but he didn't like me leaving the house.

Sometimes, it was easier to do what he said than argue with him and his stranger-danger logic."

"Telecommute, eh? Why do I get the feeling your fake grandfather has made you somewhat of a recluse?

I frowned. "I'm not a recluse."

"You also don't have much of a life, from the sound of it."

"I have friends that I see occasionally, and I go to the library pretty frequently. I'm not a shut-in."

He coughed out, "Recluse."

I glared at him. "Well, what do you do, Cam the solitude-hating cambion?"

"I'm self-employed."

"What kind of work?" I asked.

He clenched his jaw, looking like he'd rather talk about anything else.

"Come on. It can't be that bad."

"I'm an escort," he said finally. "Women pay me to 'take them out.'"

"Take them out? Wait a minute. You steal souls and get paid for it? That's a little diabolical, isn't it?"

He waved his hand back and forth. "Yes and no."

"Yes and no, it's diabolical? Or yes, you steal souls, and no, you don't get paid for it?"

"I could deplete a human's soul over a few visits if I chose to be that big of a douchebag," he explained. "But I can't take all of it in one go. Not like my father can. And yes, I do get paid for sex, if that's what my clients want."

"Do any of your clients ever not want to have sex with you?"

He raised an eyebrow. "What do you think?"

Hugging one of the thin, but thankfully clean, bed pillows to my chest, I answered, "Honestly, I think you probably fuck a lot, Cam."

His smile was pure, unadulterated sex. "You're not wrong."

I laughed nervously. "I guess you really are your father's son."

"That I am," he said, regarding me with a look of interest.

I ignored the close examination and asked, "But you're not all incubus, right? What's your mom's half?"

"Human. Cambions are the sons and daughters of an incubus father and a human mother."

"Really? Is she in your life?"

"She died when I was six years old."

"I'm so sorry."

He waved away my concern. "It was many, many years ago, and truthfully, I was lucky to have the time I did have with her. Human women rarely survive mating with an incubus in their true form. The insemination can be violent, and the pregnancy fatal. My father was stupid to try for more offspring with her."

The angry vehemence in his voice made me flinch away from him. Noticing the movement, he said, "My father is not a topic I enjoy discussing. He is the biggest asshole I know."

"Only because you haven't spent much time with my 'grandfather,'" I grumbled.

He chuckled. "I'd say it's a demon thing, but then we'd be included in this demons-are-douchebags theory."

I unfolded my legs and scooted to the edge of the bed. "Speaking of being a demon, do you have a different form? You know, something more demon-y, or do you always look like this?"

Cam swung his legs off the bed and mimicked my position. "For a girl that was only a human yesterday, I would have thought you'd be afraid to see what a demon looks like."

"That was yesterday," I said. "Today, I'm the Exitium Daemonium, and I'm running for my life. Things have changed a bit."

He nodded. "I guess they have."

"So, let's see it. Demon out or whatever."

"Demon out?" he asked, a slight smile playing on his lips. "Sorry to disappoint, but this is my only form. If I were a true, full-blooded incubus, I could be anything you desire, male or female."

My mouth dropped open. "Anything?"

"Anything. An incubus can sense what you want and shape-shift accordingly. They'll do anything they have to, to take a soul."

"Then I'm kind of glad I don't have a soul."

"No, but you have other things an incubus, or even I, could take from you."

My breath quickened as I stared into his eyes. The shade of brown was so mesmerizing; I immediately lost myself in the flecks of dark chocolate and warm amber. "Cam, you're . . ."

"I'm what?" he asked, his gruff voice so close to my ear, I jumped.

Blinking fast, I pulled away from Cam with no memory of how I'd left my bed to join him on his.

"What just . . ." I trailed off again, staring at Cameron. His full lips looked so soft, yielding but firm at the same time. I wondered, if he kissed me, if I would feel the warm jolt I'd felt before when he touched me. I wondered if I'd feel it everywhere he touched me.

"Mavis!" he said sharply.

Coming back to myself, I shook my head to clear it. "What did you do to me?"

"I let you feel me in my natural state."

With my heart pounding, I scrambled back to my bed. "That was your natural state?"

He shot me a rueful smile. "You're still being throttled by the magic device around your heart. My charm shouldn't affect an ice demon, or any demon for that matter. Whatever that device around your heart is, it's cracked, but clearly still doing its job. The only question is if your power will be limited by the throttle permanently or if the break will slowly trickle magic into you until you're whole again."

"So, the more magic I develop, the less I'll be affected by your . . . um, charm?"

"I'm sorry, yes. You don't know how much I wish I could turn it completely off—the want, the desire. I'm holding it back as much as I can."

"I don't want you to turn it off," I said, surprising myself.

His brows lifted. "No?"

I smiled, thinking of how my body felt when I looked into his eyes. "No way. Giving myself over to your hypnotism, or whatever it is, feels decadent, delicious, like sliding into a hot bath at the end of the day. I like it. A lot."

"Yeah?" he asked.

"Yeah," I purred, matching his tone. "And that warm lick of sexual electricity you send through my body when you touch me? It's heaven."

"I like the way you describe that," he said, in a voice that could be considered foreplay. "It has a lot of my favorite words in it."

"Oh?" I asked. "Like what?"

"It has warm, and lick, and . . ."

"And what?" I asked, hanging on to every word.

"And sexual electricity."

The sound of him growling out the word *sexual* made me grab the edge of the mattress with both hands to brace myself. I swallowed hard. "Holy shit, Cam. You're really good at this seduction thing."

Cameron groaned and shifted his hips, drawing my attention downward. I gasped. He was hard—and massive. My eyes snapped back up to his.

Panic crossed his beautiful face for a split second. "Don't, Mavis."

"Don't what?" I asked, my voice barely above a whisper.

"Give in to the desire. You must resist this."

Nearly breathless with a need that was as unfamiliar as it was overwhelming, I asked, "Why?"

"Because I don't know if I can tell you no."

Purchase *Plans Laid Bare* wherever books are sold.